Babysitting the Baumgartners

By Selena Kitt

Babysitting the Baumgartners © 2008 Selena Kitt
Cover Photo Credit: Jess Cruz
Used under a Creative Commons license.
Cover Design: Selena Kitt
eXcessica publishing
All rights reserved

To order additional copies of this book contact:
books@excessica.com

Young people are in a condition like permanent intoxication, because youth is sweet and they are growing...

—Aristotle

The sexual life of adult women is a dark continent...
—Freud

Prologue

I was fifteen when I started babysitting for the Baumgartners. They had two kids. Henry and Janie were four and five the first time I sat in their living room eating pizza and watching "Lilo and Stitch" with them. I still remember them that way, both conked out on the floor, their greasy faces smearing their mom's white carpet.

I loved babysitting for them. Mr. Baumgartner—"Call me Doc, everybody does"—usually came home drunk enough to pay me way too much for the night. Mrs. Baumgartner—she never said to call her anything but Mrs. Baumgartner, although I did shorten it to "Mrs. B" over the years—was very pretty and very nice and kept really good ice cream (Häagen-Dazs) in the freezer. They had a huge TV, an enormous house, and I became their regular babysitter every Friday night, sometimes Saturdays, too, all through high school.

My parents complained they never saw me on weekends, and would ask "Where are you going now?" as I headed out the door, calling back, "I'm babysitting the Baumgartners!"

"Again?"

Mr. and Mrs. B liked to go out. And I liked the magazines and clothes I could buy with all my extra babysitting money. I never had to flip burgers like my sister, Amy. The Baumgartners even sold me my first car, a 2001 Saturn, at a price far less than I would have been given anywhere else—Mrs. B said Doc was just tired of picking me up and driving me home.

I used to have my little sister, Amy, go babysit whenever I had a conflict. That usually meant I had a date—and the Baumgartners hated it when I started dating. Really, it was a hardship for me, too. Tough call—a date with Toby Lumetto, or babysitting the Baumgartners? Amy complained the kids never behaved for her, but they always did for me. They were great kids.

I loved the Baumgartners and they loved me.

The winter of the year I graduated high school, the Baumgartners went to Key West. When they came back, Mrs. Baumgartner swore she'd never do it again without help. Henry was seven and Janie was eight, and they were "too much of a handful," she said. Just kids, I thought, but I wasn't their parent—I was pretty much their playmate—so what did I know?

The next winter, Mrs. Baumgartner called and asked if I wanted to come with them—all expenses paid, over the Christmas holiday—a free trip to Key West! It took me about five seconds to say "Yes!" to that proposition. My parents hemmed and hawed about it, but I was over eighteen by then, and I could pretty much do what I wanted...technically. I finally got their blessing, packed my bags, and we were off to the land of sunshine and bikinis!

Up until then, I'd sort of thought of the Baumgartners as surrogate parents, but it was during the trip to Key West when things changed. The Baumgartners became more to me—much more—and that wasn't all that changed. Everything changed that summer.

If I'd known... I don't know. But I had no idea at the time how transformative the trip would be, then and even later in my life.

Chapter One

December in the Midwest wasn't exactly tanning weather, and I wanted to come back and show off, sleek and brown as a seal. I had a bathing suit, of course, yellow and white, fairly respectable, since I was going to be taking the kids to the beach. It did have a bikini top but boy-shorts bottoms. I left the micro-suit at home. I figured Mrs. Baumgartner wouldn't approve.

Shows you what I knew.

The morning after we arrived, Mrs. Baumgartner came out and joined me on the beach. I was supervising the kids, who were busy making some sort of sand castle—really, it was more of a sand village, as it already spanned half the beach! What I was really doing was trying to read a Nora Roberts novel while simultaneously working on my nonexistent tan, but I was bored.

That ended the minute Mrs. Baumgartner walked out of the house. I glanced up as she slid the door wall closed behind her, and I was glad she paused to look at her reflection in the glass, working to pull her long blonde hair up into a ponytail, because my jaw practically hit the sand. I didn't know what she would have said about me wearing the little white micro-bikini I'd left in my drawer at home, but for a moment, I simply couldn't hide my shock when Mrs. Baumgartner stepped out of the house wearing her own black micro-suit!

No one out here to see here – why not? I rationalized it as I watched her adjust the bikini strings. The house was right on the ocean and we had a private beach. Mr. Baumgartner said it was a timeshare. Henry and Janie had wanted to swim immediately and, it felt like, all the time, so I'd already spent tons of hours trying to soak up some sun. My skin was pale next to Mrs. Baumgartner's though, and for the life of me, I couldn't see a tan line on her body. Of course, her backside was completely exposed in her suit, and the front covered...very little.

I averted my eyes as she laid out a large blanket on the white sand next to my towel. "How are you feeling, Veronica?" She was the only one who ever called me by my full name. Everyone else called me "Ronnie."

"Better." I put my book down and turned over onto my back. We'd ordered pizza the night before, after we'd unpacked, and something on it hadn't agreed with me. I shaded my eyes and looked over at the kids. They were now having a sand fight, screeching and throwing shovels of the white stuff at each other. I sighed. I knew someone was gonna start screaming any minute about sand in their eyes or their suit, and then I'd have to go to work.

"Henry and Janie, you need to go in the house!" Mrs. Baumgartner called, stretching out on her stomach on the blanket.

"I can take care of them, Mrs. B." Her bikini thong left her bronzed, rounded bottom completely exposed. I blinked fast and looked away. "That's what I'm here for, right?"

The kids stopped at their mother's warning and treaded through the sand toward us. They really were great kids. I wished sometimes my sisters and I got along as well as they did.

"Why don't you two go inside?" Mrs. Baumgartner said as they approached. "There's lunch on the counter, and Daddy hooked up the X-Box."

"Woot!" Henry whooped, kicking up sand as he headed for the door wall. Janie didn't look as thrilled, but the promise of lunch was enough to lure her into the house.

"You know, watching the kids isn't all you're here for, Veronica." Mrs. Baumgartner turned her face to me after they went in, resting her cheek on her folded arms. "Doc and I were just talking last night about how much you've done for us over the years. The kids adore you. You're like part of the family."

I flushed. "Thanks."

"You deserve a good vacation." She smiled, her eyes creasing at the corners. I wondered how old she was. It was hard for me to judge how old people were—to me, they just seemed either old or young. Mrs. B wasn't really either. "It's the least we can do."

"If I can get a tan, that will be reward enough." I grabbed the oil next to my towel and poured some into my hands. I worked more of it into my thighs and over my smooth, flat belly. I noticed her watching me. "Do you want some?"

"Sure." She took the bottle and sat up to squeeze a pool of glistening liquid into her palm, rubbing it over her shoulders and arms. I slipped my boy short bottoms aside, checking for a tan line. I actually had one, which was thrilling, although it wasn't as dark as I wanted it to be.

"You can take it off." Mrs. Baumgartner untied her black bikini top around the neck and I stared as she started to spread oil over her full, naked breasts.

I knew I was staring, but I couldn't help it. Her skin was smooth and tawny—even there. Her nipples were brown, vastly different from my light pink ones.

"Wh—what?" I stammered. I was still staring. She smoothed oil over her belly, which was softer and a little more rounded than mine, working it under the strings of her bikini and down into the grooves of her thighs.

"Your top." She massaged oil into her thighs and calves. "You can take it off—so you won't have any tan lines."

She lay on her back on the blanket, glancing over at me. I must have looked shocked. "No one can see, Veronica. It's a private beach—just us."

"What about the kids?" I looked over my shoulder at the house.

"One word: X-Box." She adjusted herself, opening her thighs a little. I couldn't see a hint of hair under the triangle of cloth between her legs and wondered at it. Her body was fuller than mine, more rounded and soft. "I won't look. Don't be shy."

Her eyes stayed closed and I hesitated, looking up and down the beach. Then I pulled my top aside and checked my tan line—I was definitely getting one! Mrs. B's breasts were so large that they kind of sloped off to the side when she leaned back. I was a little intimidated—mine were nowhere near as big—but it was the smooth, almost bronze color of her flesh that really convinced me. I wanted a tan without lines, too!

I untied my top and slipped it off, reaching for the oil. Squeezing some into my hands, I leaned back and rubbed it into the swell of my breasts. It felt strange to be outside half-naked in full daylight—I hadn't gone topless on a beach since I was Janie's age. My nipples were small, pale pink pebbles on a puffy, rounded areola, and with the stimulation from my hands rubbing the oil on and the gentle breeze blowing in from the ocean, they were quite hard.

Mrs. B hummed something to herself, but I didn't know the tune. The rhythmic sound of the waves against the shore had me drifting in and out. Far away, I heard a dog bark.

The heat of the sun made me sweat, and I felt it mixing with the oil and trickling down my sides. It beaded between my breasts. When I snuck a look over at Mrs. B, I noticed the same thing, only it was more pronounced on her already tanned skin. I adjusted myself on the towel, straightening out the edges where they had blown up at the corners.

Mrs. B shaded her eyes and peered at me with a smile. "Why don't you come over here? There's plenty of room on the blanket and a lot less sand." I considered it for a moment and then stood, hopping from my little towel over to the larger blanket so as not to get too much sand on my feet. Settling down beside her on my back, I felt the heat from her skin, but we weren't touching.

"You have lovely breasts," she murmured, and I felt her shoulder pressing against mine where it hadn't been a moment ago.

"Th—thanks." I was glad it was so warm to hide my flush. What did you say to someone who said that? "You do, too."

"I wish I still had the body of a nineteen-year-old." She gave a sad little laugh. "So firm and tight. There's not a crease or a wrinkle on you, is there?"

Now I was really flushing. "I think you have a beautiful body. When I have two kids, I hope I can still wear a bikini out on the beach. And a micro one, at that!"

She turned her face to mine, smiling at me. "Well, thank you for the compliment." I saw her eyes move down over my breasts, and I was aware of how hard my nipples were.

The conversation was making me feel dizzy and very warm. Maybe it was the heat—but I was pretty sure it was the conversation—that, and the fact I was lying half-naked next to Mrs. Baumgartner, her thigh now pressing against mine. She'd always been friendly and flirty with me—she was that way with everyone. But this was different. Very different. Our flesh was slick and oily together when she shifted, and it sent a gentle pulse beating between my legs, keeping a fast time against the sound of the waves on the shoreline.

"Do you have a micro-bikini?" Mrs. B's eyes were closed again. I stared at her body, the generous swell of her copper-colored flesh, her big, dark nipples. Hers were hard, too.

"Yeah," I said. "But I left it at home. I didn't think it would be... appropriate."

"You can borrow one of mine." Her thigh slid along mine as she adjusted on the blanket. "If you want less of a tan line. I brought several."

"Thanks." I watched her breasts rising and falling, glistening in the sun. Her belly was beaded with sweat and oil.

"Do you shave?"

"Wh—what?"

"Do you shave?" she repeated, opening one eye to look at me. "I wax, myself. It's much easier and takes care of things for a lot longer down there, if you know what I mean."

"No." I snapped my eyes closed.

"Oh, to wear a micro, you just have to." She half-sat and touched my thigh, pulling my bathing suit bottoms aside a little to reveal the line of dark pubic hair. "Yep, you'd definitely need to shave. Or I brought some wax. You could wax it all. I do."

Shocked, I stared at her. I didn't know what I was more surprised by, her revelation or the fact she'd just nonchalantly pulled my bikini aside!

"It's actually fun." She winked. "Not the waxing part—but having a shaved pussy."

I stared right up at the sun, blinking a few times so it made bright spots in the dark when I closed my eyes. I couldn't believe Mrs. Baumgartner had just said the word "pussy" in front of me!

"Doc loves it." I felt her hand against my hip, just resting there. "And it's so incredible to walk around that way. You feel so exposed. It's a constant turn-on."

"Mrs. B..." I wasn't even sure what I wanted to say.

"I'd be happy to help you." Her fingers moved over the elastic tops of my bikini bottoms. "It's hard to do a bikini wax on yourself."

I put my arms up over my head, tilting my head back and looking around as if someone might be there to overhear this crazy conversation—someone I might share my astonishment with.

"You think about it." Her hand lightly stroked my side. I felt that gentle throbbing between my thighs, more insistent now.

"Okay," was all I could say.

There was someone on the balcony, high above us. It was Mr. Baumgartner—Doc—sitting outside on one of the white deck chairs. He was completely naked. When I got over that shock, I noticed his hand moving up and down between his legs—very fast.

Was he? *Is he?*

Mr. B's hand was warm against my side, just resting there. It made my breasts tingle, and I flushed when I realized I wanted her to touch them—to touch me. I wanted to close my eyes and my mind against the thought, but the blur of motion above drew my attention again. I knew I shouldn't be watching, but I couldn't help it.

Could he see us? I wondered. Was he up there, touching himself, looking down at his wife and the babysitting, lying topless on the beach together?

That's when he stood. I nearly gasped out loud as I watched thick, white streams of fluid erupt from the tip of his engorged cock and splash down onto the balcony and the railing.

His eyes never left mine.

"Mrs. B." My voice trembled as I sat up. "I'm gonna go cool off. I'll be right back."

I stood, not sure I could stand, but I did, forgetting I was topless. I walked, a little unsteady, toward the water and waded out into the cool waves, up to my neck. When I looked back, Mr. Baumgartner was gone, but Mrs. B was still watching me, shading her eyes from the sun.

When she waved, I waved back, feeling that steady, rhythmic pulse between my thighs. The coolness of the water only served to make the heat between my legs more pronounced. I floated on my back, watching the clouds drift, letting the waves rock me and once in a while overtake me. When I finally had the courage to get out, Mrs. B had gone into the house, and the beach was empty again.

Chapter Two

When I came back in the house, Henry and Janie were fighting over the X-Box controller, remains of lunch—peanut butter and jelly—still smeared on their faces. The air conditioning was on, and it was very cool compared to outside. I actually got goose bumps within minutes of walking in the door.

"Where's your mom and dad?"

Janie looked up at me, and Henry took the opportunity to yank the controller from her. "Hey!" she protested. "They're upstairs taking a nap. They told us to stay here until you got back in the house."

Henry started the game, and while Janie was pouting, she was also relenting, getting involved in whatever was happening on the screen.

"Well, what do you guys want to do?" No answer—just blank stares at the television. "Looks like X-Box wins. I'm going to go take a shower, okay?"

They both nodded, their mouths partly open as they stared at the screen. *Little video game zombies.* At eight and nine, they were pretty self-sufficient. I didn't understand why Mrs. Baumgartner had such a hard time with them, really. To me, they seemed like easy kids.

I climbed the stairs and went down the hall toward the bathroom. They had a large Jacuzzi tub—which I was dying to soak in one night—and a separate shower. I turned on the water, adjusting the temperature, and peeled off my suit, tossing it into the sink. It felt good to soap up and wash the oil and salt water off my body.

I stood under the needling spray for a long time. Every time I closed my eyes, I saw Mr. Baumgartner's hand moving, lightning fast, up and down the length of his cock. It gave me a tight, funny feeling in my belly. That throbbing between my legs hadn't quit.

When I slipped the soap between my thighs, rubbing it over the soft, curly hair there, I remembered what Mrs. B said about waxing and flushed. I didn't have much hair to begin with, just a sparse, dark triangular patch. What would it feel like to be completely smooth?

I slipped my fingers past my swollen lips, remembering how soft and slick Mrs. B's oiled-up thigh was against mine, how dark and hard her nipples. My clit ached at the thought and I touched it, rubbing it slowly under my fingers.

The image which kept coming back to me, though, was Mr. Baumgartner and his cock—his eyes locked on mine as he came. It made me embarrassed and excited to know seeing me and his wife lying together on the beach topless was enough to get him aroused— *to get him off.* Was he imagining something, or just watching us, or both?

I knew I shouldn't be thinking about it, but I couldn't help it. The more I thought about it, the faster my fingers moved over my clit. Leaning back against the tiles, I rubbed and rubbed it. The water made my nipples tingle. The images of the afternoon flashed through my mind—Mrs. B's fingers pulling my bikini aside to look at my pubic hair, the swell and shift of her heavy breasts, the way the oil and water pooled on her tanned skin, the way her eyes lingered on my chest and belly and thighs.

Moaning softly, I slipped one finger inside my pussy, rocking against my hand and feeling a low hum building in my lower belly. That steady throb between my legs which had begun outside in the sun was like a fast, heavy drumbeat now keeping time with my pounding heart. Was he really watching us that whole time? Could he hear us? How long had he been sitting there, stroking himself?

The sight of his cock, bursting like a spewing geyser over his fist, the pleasure on his face, the way his eyes met mine—oh God, I couldn't stand it. I shuddered and moaned and arched against the tiles as I came, remembering his dark eyes, his pumping hand, his bucking hips and spurting cock.

Flushed from my orgasm and the heat of the shower, I knelt in the tub, turning off the water. I rested my hot cheek against the cool tile for a moment, closing my eyes and feeling the waves of pleasure slowly receding. I felt shy and embarrassed to see him, now, wondering what I would say, what he might say.

When my legs felt steady enough to hold me, I got out of the shower and dried off, wrapping myself in one of the big white bath sheets. My room was across the hall from the bathroom, and the Baumgartner's was the next room over. The kids' rooms were at the other end of the hallway.

As I made my way across the hall, I heard Mrs. B's voice from behind their door. "You want that tight little nineteen-year-old pussy, Doc?"

I stopped, my heart leaping, my breath caught. *Oh my God.* Were they talking about me? He said something, but it was low, and I couldn't quite make it out. Then she said, "Just wait until I wax it for you. It'll be soft and smooth as a baby."

Shocked, I reached down between my legs, cupping my pussy as if to protect it, standing there transfixed, listening. I stepped closer to their door, seeing it wasn't completely closed, still trying to hear what they were saying. There wasn't any noise, now.

"Oh God!" I heard him groan. "Suck it harder."

My eyes wide, I felt the pulse returning between my thighs, a slow, steady heat. Was she sucking his cock? I remembered what it looked like in his hand—even from a distance, I could tell it was big—much bigger than any of the boys I'd ever been with.

"Ahhhh fuck, Carrie!" He moaned. I bit my lip, hearing Mrs. B's first name felt so wrong, somehow. "Take it all, baby!"

All?! My jaw dropped as I tried to imagine, pressing my hand over my throbbing mound. Mrs. B said something, but I couldn't hear it, and as I leaned toward the door, I bumped it with the towel wrapped around my hair. My hand went to my mouth and I took an involuntary step back as the door edged open just a crack. I turned to go to my room, but I knew that they would hear the sound of my door.

"You want to fuck me, baby?" she purred. "God, I'm so wet...did you see her sweet little tits?"

"Fuck, yeah," he murmured. "I wanted to come all over them."

Hearing his voice, I stepped back toward the door, peering through the crack. The bed was behind the door, at the opposite angle, but there was a large vanity table and mirror against the other wall, and I could see them reflected in it. Mrs. B was completely naked, kneeling over him. I saw her face, her breasts swinging as she took him into her mouth. His cock stood straight up in the air.

"She's got beautiful tits, doesn't she?" Mrs. B ran her tongue up and down the shaft.

"Yeah." His hand moved in her hair, pressing her down onto his cock. "I want to see her little pussy so bad. God, she's so beautiful."

"Do you want to see me eat it?" She moved up onto him, still stroking his cock. "Do you want to watch me lick that sweet, shaved cunt?"

I pressed a cool palm to my flushed cheek, but my other hand rubbed the towel between my legs as I watched. I'd never heard anyone say that word out loud and it both shocked and excited me.

"Oh God, yeah!" He grabbed her tits as they swayed over him. I saw her riding him, and knew he must be inside of her. "I want inside her tight little cunt."

I moved the towel aside and slipped my fingers between my lips.

He's talking about me!

The thought made my whole body tingle, and my pussy felt on fire. Already slick and wet from my orgasm in the shower, my fingers slid easily through my slit.

"I want to fuck her while she eats your pussy." He thrust up into her, his hands gripping her hips. Her breasts swayed as they rocked together. My eyes widened at the image he conjured, but Mrs. B moaned, moving faster on top of him.

"Yeah, baby!" She leaned over, her breasts dangling in his face. His hands went to them, his mouth sucking at her nipples, making her squeal and slam down against him even harder. "You want her on her hands and knees, her tight little ass in the air?"

He groaned, and I rubbed my clit even faster as he grabbed her and practically threw her off him onto the bed. She seemed to know what he wanted, because she got onto her hands and knees and he fucked her like that, from behind. The sound of them, flesh slapping against flesh, filled the room.

They were turned toward the mirror, but Mrs. B had her face buried in her arms, her ass lifted high in the air. Doc's eyes looked down between their legs, like he was watching himself slide in and out of her.

"Fuck!" Mrs. B's voice was muffled. "Oh fuck, Doc! Make me come!"

He grunted and drove into her harder. I watched her shudder and grab the covers in her fists. He didn't stop, though—his hands grabbed her hips and he worked himself into her over and over. I felt weak-kneed and full of heat, my fingers rubbing my aching clit in fast little circles. Mrs. B's orgasm had almost sent me right over the edge. I was very, very close.

"That tight nineteen-year-old cunt!" He shoved into her. "I want to taste her." He slammed into her again. "Fuck her." And again. "Make her come." And again. "Make her scream until she can't take anymore."

I leaned my forehead against the doorjamb for support, trying to control how fast my breath was coming, how fast my climax was coming, but I couldn't. I whimpered, watching him fuck her and knowing he was imagining me...*me!*

"Come here." He pulled out and Mrs. B turned around like she knew what he wanted. "Swallow it."

He knelt up on the bed as she pumped and sucked at his cock. I saw the first spurt land against her cheek, a thick white strand of cum, and then she covered the head with her mouth and swallowed, making soft mewing noises in her throat. I came then, too, shuddering and shivering against the doorframe, biting my lip to keep from crying out.

When I opened my eyes and came to my senses, Mrs. B was still on her hands and knees, focused between his legs—but Doc was looking right at me, his dark eyes on mine.

He saw me. For the second time today—he saw me.

My hand flew to my mouth and I stumbled back, fumbling for the doorknob behind me I knew was there. I finally found it, slipping into my room and shutting the door behind me. I leaned against it, my heart pounding, my pussy dripping, and wondered what I was going to do now.

Chapter Three

I buried my red, flushed face into the coolness of my pillow and decided I wasn't going to leave my room. I just couldn't face them, after what had happened. When Mrs. B knocked on my door for dinner, I told her I wasn't feeling well again.

"Anything I can get you?" she asked kindly.

I shook my head and called a muffled, "No!" into my pillow.

Downstairs, they played games, talking, laughing. I heard Janie and Henry fighting over the X-Box again, but then Doc turned it off and put in Monty Python, which had them both laughing hysterically. It wasn't something I thought I'd let my eight and nine year old watch, but I wasn't their parent, what did I know? I was just the babysitter.

Some babysitter—hiding up in her room! I just couldn't imagine looking into his eyes, knowing he had seen me masturbating in their doorway while I watched them have sex. What must he think of me, now?

My face burned at the thought, but the images of them together kept coming back to me, again and again. I couldn't stop remembering how her breasts had swayed when he pounded into her, how she had turned around to swallow his cum, like she couldn't get enough.

I wasn't a virgin, but all of my experiences with boys had been mostly basement or back seat fumblings, quick and mildly pleasurable. I'd never heard or seen anything like what Mr. and Mrs. B were doing in their bedroom this afternoon.

I was so lost in my own world I didn't even bother to get dressed. I just tossed my wet towel on the floor and curled up under the covers. I think I drifted off. The heat of the sun had made me sleepy and a little lethargic.

My dreams were about Doc, seeing him stroking his cock over my breasts, rubbing the fat, bulbous tip over my hard, pink nipples. He kept whispering, "I want to come all over you, Ronnie. I want to come all over your sweet little tits."

When I woke up, my pussy throbbed with the images from my dream, the light had faded to near-dim, and I couldn't hear the kids anymore. Someone knocked at my door, and I realized that was what must have woken me.

"Come in."

It was Mrs. B, and she carried a cup of tea she set next to me on the night table. I felt her hand in my hair, brushing it away from my eyes.

"How are you feeling?" She sat on the edge of the bed behind me.

"A little better." I turned my face to her.

"I brought you some tea," she said, and I felt her weight shifting.

"Thanks."

"What hurts?" she asked. "Is it your tummy?" I nodded, closing my eyes as she traced her fingers over my forehead. "Here, move over." I stiffened for a moment, feeling her curling herself around me. "Let me rub it. Sometimes it helps."

"Mrs. B," I whispered, but her hand slid over the comforter, massaging my belly through the material.

She smelled sweet, and I knew she must have taken a shower, too, after sunbathing. We'd both been so oiled up and sweaty. Remembering how she looked, rubbing oil into her breasts and then lying topless next to me, made me shiver.

"Better?" she murmured, her mouth close to my ear.

I shook my head. "No."

"Well, here." She slid her hand under the covers. "Maybe like this." I swallowed hard as Mrs. B's hand slid below my navel, rubbing the taut, flat surface of my belly. She was gentle, tender, rubbing it in slow, easy circles.

"Is it your period?" Her fingers moved a little further down. They touched the top of my pubic hair now.

"No."

She continued to knead my flesh, and I felt her breath against my cheek. Her arm brushed across the side of my breast with her motion, making me tingle. She must have known I was completely naked under the covers.

I turned a little toward her, and now my nipple rubbed against her upper arm as she moved her fingers lower, bit by bit. Her hand slipped over my pubic bone. I felt my breath coming faster and tried to control it. Her breasts pressed tight against my back. I felt the generous swell and shift of them when she moved.

"Better yet?" She kissed my cheek. The light had grown dimmer, and I could barely see her outline now, but I felt the weight and heat of her behind me.

"A little." I shifted on the bed and felt her fingers dip between my already swollen, wet lips. Gasping, I pulled away from her hand.

"It's okay." She put her whole hand over my mound. "This might make you feel better."

I drew a shaky breath. Her hand just massaged me, covering my lips, her fingers not moving inside. I sighed, closing my eyes. It felt so good I could barely stand it. Her arm moved over my nipple as she worked her hand slowly between my legs. I let out a little moan, squirming under her.

I turned a little more towards her. Her mouth was right there, so close I felt her breath on my face. She smelled of beer or alcohol, and something sweet that was just the scent of her. "I have to tell you something."

"What is it?" Her palm rocked between my thighs. I gasped, biting my lip to keep from crying out. My pussy was wet and throbbing and aching for some sort of release. She pressed her cheek to mine, and her lips were soft there, inches from my own.

"This afternoon..." I moaned when she started making circles between my legs, moving her hand around and around on my mound and rubbing the flesh of my lips over the sensitive bud of my clit.

"Yes?" she encouraged, moving her hand a little faster.

"Oh, God," I whispered against her cheek, shivering. "Please."

"What is it, Veronica?"

When I closed my eyes, I saw Doc fucking her, plunging his cock into her from behind. It sent a jolt straight between my legs.

"I saw you," I confessed quickly. "This afternoon, in your room... you and Doc..."

Her hand slowed, and I felt a thick pulse throbbing under her fingers. "I know, sweetie...it's okay."

I could barely breathe. "You know?"

"Yes." Her lips pressed against the side of my mouth as she talked, and I felt their softness, their tender movement against my skin. "Doc told me. He saw you."

"Oh God." I moaned, not sure if it was in embarrassment or pleasure.

"Shhhh." She rubbed her lips over mine, not really a kiss, more just a caress. "It's going to be ok."

Her hand moved between my legs again. I whimpered. "Oh, please."

A knock sounded at the door and we both jumped. I pulled the covers up to my chin and Mrs. B sat up on the bed.

"Come in," I called.

The door opened, spilling light from the hallway. It was Doc, his large frame filling the doorway.

"How're my girls?" He leaned against the door frame.

I blushed. "Okay. I'm feeling a little better. Mrs. B brought me some tea."

He came over and sat on the other side of the bed, putting his hand on my hip. "Glad to hear it. It's no good being sick on vacation. You're here to have fun."

"Yeah." I agreed, feeling his big hand massaging my hip through the blanket. It sent tingles straight into my pelvis where my pussy was still wet and aching from Mrs. B's massage.

"You get some rest." He moved his fingers under my chin. "You'll feel better tomorrow."

"Thanks," I murmured, almost sad when he moved his hand and stood.

"Come on, Carrie." He held out his hand. "Let's get to bed and let her rest."

Mrs. B stood, following her husband. "Good night."

"Thank you," I called as they went out, shutting the door.

I breathed a deep sigh, staring up at the ceiling in the darkness. I didn't know what to think, what to feel. I rolled over onto my belly, hugging my pillow, my pussy burning between my thighs, aching to be touched. I tried to ignore it and sleep, but the more I did, the more restless I became.

I heard Mr. and Mrs. B laughing and talking in their bedroom. I tossed and turned on the bed, trying to find a cool spot, a comfortable position.

Finally, I got up, deciding to draw a bath. Tonight was as good a night as any to try out that big Jacuzzi tub. I pulled my robe on and found my towel on the floor. It was still damp, so I hung it over the end of the bed, deciding to get a new one from the linen closet.

"That's the taste of her pussy, baby." I heard Mrs. B's voice when I peeked out my door. I saw a light on in their room, coming from a crack in the door. "Go ahead, taste it."

"Oh my God," he murmured, and I closed my eyes, hearing a sucking sound. "You had your fingers in her?"

"Not quite," Mrs. B said. "Almost. I was just...rubbing her ouchie tummy for her."

Doc chuckled. "God, she tastes so good. I want to eat that sweet little cunt."

Flushing, I pressed my hand between my legs, feeling the incredible heat there. I knew they were talking about me.

"Me first, Doc," Mrs. B pouted. "I want to taste her, too."

I closed my eyes, slipping a hand under the soft flap of my robe and dipping a finger between my swollen lips. Shivering when I touched my clit, I let my fingers stay there for a moment, nudging it a little.

"We can share," Doc replied, his voice low.

I heard sucking sounds again and stepped out of my door and a little closer to theirs. The door was open just a little bit again and I could see them in the mirror. Mrs. B straddled his belly and he sucked greedily at her fingers.

Flushing, a heat spreading over my chest, I realized he was tasting my juices on her fingers. Curious, I lifted my own fingers to my mouth, sucking on them quietly. It was a musky tang that coated my throat when I swallowed. Is that what every woman tasted like? I wondered. Is that what Mrs. B tasted like? Oh my God, I couldn't believe I was even thinking about it. I backed away from the door, determined to go take my bath and leave them their privacy.

"Do you really think she'll do it?" I heard Doc ask. I stopped, closing my eyes.

"I think so," Mrs. B replied, her voice muffled. I turned back to the door, leaning in to see her kneeling between his legs now, his cock moving in and out of her mouth.

Do what? I wondered, watching in fascination as he disappeared between her lips over and over. As she sucked him, I found myself aching to know what his cock felt like in my mouth. His hands moved in her hair, pressing her down further and further.

"God, I hope so!" He groaned as she came up on his cock, licking around the tip like an ice cream cone. My fingers found their way between my fleshy lips, searching for my aching clit and finding it. "Now that I've tasted that sweet little pussy, I want more."

"You'll have to settle for mine tonight," she purred, moving up and straddling his face.

"You're never settling, sweetie."

I watched, my eyes wide, as he grabbed her hips and she began to grind, moaning. She rocked and rocked on him, her heavy breasts swaying. Her fingers found her own nipples, rolling them, her head going back, her long blonde hair brushing his chest.

My breath came fast, and I lifted my fingers up to my own nipples, squeezing and rolling them like she was. The sensation sent heat through my whole body, making my pussy buzz with delicious warmth. I wished I had three hands as I kept one tweaking my nipple and slid the other back down between my legs.

Oh God, my pussy was so wet! I wanted to come, hard and fast, but I didn't want to stop watching them. Mrs. B trembled, calling his name and saying things I'd never heard anyone say out loud before.

"Yes!" she moaned. "Eat my cunt, baby. Oh fuck, don't stop!"

I heard him, muffled, between her thighs, and wondered how he could possibly even breathe. His hand was between his own legs, shuttling up and down the length of his cock. I didn't know where to look— her swaying breasts and rocking hips, or his hard, red cock, just starting to get wet at the tip.

"Ohhh God!" she cried. "I'm gonna come all over your face!"

I bit my lip, easing up on my clit just a little, or I would have come with her right then. She shuddered and leaned her palms against the wall above her head to catch herself. I noticed Doc squeezing his cock hard, groaning between her legs, and I heard her wetness, or maybe it was the sound of his mouth on her. Either way, it made me dizzy with lust.

"Oh God." Her body shook as she climbed off of him. "You have the best tongue, Doc."

"Is that all you want me for?" He chuckled, his hand stroking again, lazy. I nudged my clit with my finger, back and forth, as I watched him.

"No," she purred, moving his hand out of the way and stroking him herself. "You have the best cock, too."

"Good enough to eat?"

"Always." She moved down and took him back into her mouth. Her body was in the way, and I couldn't see his cock in the mirror anymore. I stretched on my tiptoes, straining to see past her bottom. It was up in the air, and I saw her lips, completely bare, just like she said they were. They were slick and glistening in the lamplight.

"Yeah, baby!" He moaned, and I saw his hand pressing her head down again. She was almost gagging on him but didn't seem to mind. "Deeper... come on... you can do it."

She moaned and her ass wiggled back and forth. As I watched, she slipped her hand between her legs and began to massage her smooth lips, round and round, just like she had rubbed me in the bedroom earlier.

I opened my robe a little more, bending over to look down between my legs at the dark triangle there. Making my palm flat over it, I began to rub, round and round. The sensation reminded me of her hand moving between my thighs and I leaned against the doorframe, rubbing faster as I watched.

Doc bucked up into her mouth on the bed, grunting and moaning, louder and louder. I whimpered, easing back on my rubbing a little, wanting it to last forever. I wanted to see him come again. From this angle, though, I knew I couldn't, and from the sounds of it, he was going to fill her mouth and make her swallow it again.

Almost like he knew, suddenly he was sitting up, rolling her over onto the bed and spreading her legs apart with his thighs. I could see everything now, the tip of his cock rubbing up and down her slick slit before he slid into her, his hips rocking as he held himself above her.

"Fuck me!" she growled, and I saw her hands digging hard into his ass, pulling him deeper into her. "You like that wet cunt squeezed around you, baby?"

He groaned, moving faster, driving deeper, and I felt myself edging near a point of no return. My fingers wouldn't stop moving against the tender bud of my clit, making delicious circles there, and my nipples were hard and poking straight out. I used my other hand to tweak them, first one, then the other.

"Ahhhh God!" I saw him thrust even faster, pumping in and out of her now. "I'm gonna come!"

"Come all over me!" She groaned as he pulled out. I saw her fingers working her pussy, round and round, just like me. His cock throbbed and twitched, sending huge jets of his cum over her bare, swollen mound. A thick, white cascade of it slipped between her lips and ran down toward the mattress.

I stared at that flood of cum and wondered how it would taste, mixed with all her tangy juices. I trembled all over, feeling my orgasm taking me, shuddering through me with a force that threatened to buckle my knees. Lifting my fingers to my mouth and sucking on them, I moved quickly away from the door, heading for the bathroom.

When I locked the door and started running the water in the tub, I took off my robe and stood in front of the mirror, wondering what Doc had meant when he said, "Do you think she'll do it?" Of course he meant me. What did he want me to do? Was it—could it possibly be—all of the naughty things I was thinking?

I closed my eyes, remembering how he grabbed her, held her, pressed her, fucked her. It made me flush and my breath came quicker. I met my own eyes in the mirror when I opened them, realizing that whatever "it" was, Mrs. B was probably right. I was going to do it.

Chapter Four

"How'd you sleep, Ronnie?" Doc came into the kitchen wearing just a pair of swim trunks, and I noticed how tanned and broad his back was as he bent down to look into the fridge.

"Good," I replied over my cup of coffee. Janie and Henry chewed mouthfuls of Cocoa Crispies and Fruity Pebbles, each reading their respective boxes with a measure of concentration I only saw when they stared at the TV. "How about you?"

"Great." He shut the fridge and poured himself a cup of coffee, grabbing a banana off the counter. "Hey, you want one of these?"

I stared at the banana in his hand and then met his eyes, swallowing and nodding. "Sure."

He sat next to me at the table, ruffling Henry's hair and tugging at Janie's ponytail as he sat down. They both mumbled some semblance of "Morning Dad," before going back to their cereal trance.

"Where's Mrs. B?" I took the banana from him and ignored the tingling feeling I got when his hand brushed mine.

"Getting her suit on." He took a big bite of his banana and chewed. "We're going for a swim. You kids want to come?"

Henry looked up from his cereal box and then over to Janie. "Okay."

At least I knew they were actually paying attention to the conversation. "Well, I guess that means I'm coming, too."

"You can get some more sun." He took another bite as he watched me peel my banana.

"Yep." I bit the inside of my cheek, avoiding his eyes, but I felt them on me. I deliberately slipped the top of the banana between my lips, licking the tip and glancing at him before taking a small bite. I heard his breath catch and tried not to smile.

"You guys coming swimming?" Mrs. B came into the kitchen in a white bikini, different from the one she'd been wearing the day before. This one covered a little more—but not much. I saw Doc's eyes sweep over her.

"Can I wear my Spiderman suit?" Henry put his bowl in the sink.

"Did you hang it up to dry?" Mrs. B turned to pour herself some coffee. Her suit was a thong, and I saw her round, tanned behind, completely exposed.

"I'll go look." He ran toward the stairs. Janie put her bowl into his in the sink with a sigh and trudged after him.

"Are you coming, Veronica?" Mrs. B sat next to her husband in the seat Henry had vacated. I nodded, taking another slow, deliberate bite of banana, my eyes shifting back over to Doc. He was definitely watching me. I chewed slowly and swallowed, feeling a slow heat spreading through my middle.

"Do you want to borrow one of my suits?" She poured cream, the white fluid turning the dark liquid a smooth tan—almost the color of her skin. "I noticed yours was still in the sink. I hung it, but I don't think it's dry yet."

"Oh!" I flushed. "I forgot it. I'm sorry."

"That's okay." She glanced over at Doc and gave him a smile. "Come on upstairs. I'll get you one of mine. Will you take the kids out when they're ready, babe?"

Doc leaned back in his chair, putting his hands behind his head. "Will do."

I put my half-eaten banana on the table, following Mrs. B upstairs. I felt Doc's eyes on us as we left the room, Mrs. B in her micro-bikini and me in my boy shorts and t-shirt.

"What color do you want?" She tossed suits out of her drawer. I stared at the selection piling up on the bed. She sat on the edge, sifting through them. "Oh, here's a good one. It's adjustable. Don't want you falling out." She winked at me, holding it up. It was a light orange color and to me it looked awfully small.

"Let's try it on." She tossed it to me. I turned my back, even though I knew she could see me in the mirror, and pulled off my shirt. The cups were large for me, of course—she was probably twice my size in that department—but it tied up top and in back, closing the gap.

"Here." She watched me struggle with the ties. "Let me." Her fingers moved lightly down my shoulder blades as she tied the strings in back. I held my long dark hair up and out of her way while she tied the ones around my neck.

"Not bad." She cocked her head and looked at me in the mirror. "What do you think?"

I turned a little, staring at my reflection. "I like it."

"Well, let's try the bottoms." She held them up.

I hooked my thumbs in my boy shorts, pulling them down over my slim hips. I saw her watching me in the mirror, looking between my thighs. I took the bikini bottoms from her, balancing on one foot as I stepped into the leg holes, which were just a configuration of strings, really, attached to a small orange patch of material. Her hips were obviously wider than mine, because the ties on the sides needed to be re-tightened.

"Here." She saw me working on one of the knots. "You keep going on that one. I'll see if I can get this one." Kneeling on the other side of me, she began to try to fumble with the knot. I did the other side. They were very tight and hard to unfasten.

"Damn thing!" She swore, and I noticed her long nails giving her a problem. Mine were shorter, but even I was having difficulty getting my side undone. It was coming—but slowly.

"Oh hell!" She leaned forward and grasped the knot in her teeth. I gasped, feeling her breath against my hip, looking down and watching her pull at the string, jerking her head as she tried to get it loose.

"Got it!" She grinned up at me and laughed. "Sometimes you have to get creative."

I smiled as she tied the string tighter around my hip. I finally unloosened mine and did the other side, adjusting the tiny orange triangle between my legs. The back was a thong, just a thin string that ran up between my cheeks. Mrs. B stayed on her knees, studying the orange material, and she began to pull it, first left, then right, frowning.

"Sweetie, I think we're going to have to do something about this." She bit her lip and tried again, this time right, then left.

"Look." She pointed to the mirror and I went to stand in front of it. "You've got just a little too much hair down there to wear it out, don't you think?"

I could see what she'd been doing now, with all her tugging. There was a line of dark, curly hair showing on one side or the other of the small stretch of material, no matter how you positioned it. It also showed a fine line of hair along the top edge, although I could pull it up to cover that.

"I guess I can't wear it." I sighed.

"Sure you can." She came up behind me, her hands on my shoulders. She turned me, pushing me gently toward the bedroom door. "Come on, we'll fix it."

She guided me into the bathroom, shutting and locking the door behind us. I heard the kids downstairs, and Doc's voice floating above them. Mrs. B took a towel out of the linen closet and spread it on the long counter which connected the twin sinks. There was a large mirror behind it and I glanced at my reflection. I liked the color on me, the way it made my just-starting-to-tan skin look a little more brown somehow.

"Ok, take those off." Mrs. B tugged at the string of the bikini bottoms. I opened my mouth to say something, but I wasn't sure what to say, so I just slid them down over my hips and left them sitting on the rug.

"Hop up." She patted the towel with a smile.

"Um... " I watched her put a razor and a can of shaving gel on the counter.

"Come on." She patted the towel again. "Don't worry, I've done this hundreds of times—and when Doc does it for me, it's always easier than if I do it myself."

I stared at her, sliding slowly up onto the fluffy white towel. "Doc...shaves you...*down there*?"

She turned on the water in the sink to my left, both hot and cold, adjusting it. "He used to—before I started to wax. But we don't really have time to wax you, not today. We'll just shave you all neat and smooth, okay?"

I nodded, not knowing what else to say. I heard the door wall opening and closing downstairs and knew they were going out. We were alone in the house.

"Easiest way to do this is for you to lean back a little and put your feet up on the counter," she instructed.

"But..." I flushed.

Sitting the way I was, or even changing in front of her, I wasn't completely exposed. Doing what she asked would spread everything wide open for her eyes and the thought made me dizzy.

"It's okay." She put her hands on my thighs, rubbing them gently up and down. Her hands were soft, her red-tipped fingers long and slender. "We're all girls here, right?"

I nodded, letting her help me as she put my feet up on the edge of the counter, resting on the towel. My back was against the mirror, and it was cold, making me shiver. At least, I *thought* that's what was making me tremble.

Mrs. B knelt between my legs, and I saw her eyes roaming over me down there. She smiled up at me and reached for the shaving cream. "You have a lovely pussy, Veronica."

I swallowed hard, not knowing what to say to that. "Will it hurt?"

"Not at all." She squirted a glob of gel into her hand and spread it over the hair between my thighs. It developed quickly into a white foamy cream. Her fingers rubbed my mound gently, making me remember how she had rubbed me last night. "It's just like shaving your legs."

She ran the razor under the stream of water before moving it toward my lips. I watched, fascinated, as she started at the top, working her way down toward my slit, rinsing the razor between swipes. She concentrated on what she was doing and seemed oblivious to the fact she was touching the most private, secret part of me.

"Open your legs a little more," she instructed as she started to shave downward, first one side and then the other. Her fingers pushed and prodded at my pussy as she went, sending sweet waves of pleasure through me. Once in a while, her hand or her fingers would nudge my clit, sending a jolt straight up my spine.

The water running down over my skin and onto the towel was warm and I closed my eyes for a moment, hearing the scrape of the razor, the running of the water, and Mrs. B's steady breathing between my legs.

I felt her breath on my thigh, even over my pussy, as she knelt there and concentrated on the work at hand. When I looked down, I saw all the dark, wiry hair which had been there since I hit puberty was now gone, leaving just a little stubble.

"This part is trickier," she said. "I've got to make it all smooth." Rinsing the blade again and then starting at the bottom, she took the razor against the grain of the hair, working her way back up my lips and over my mound. My pussy was throbbing now, and my nipples poked out of the orange bikini top, betraying my excitement.

I gasped when she spread me open with her fingers. "Mrs. B!"

"I just have to run the razor along this edge here." She pulled one of my lips taut and brought the blade up just along the inside. "I hate stray hairs, they drive me crazy. Trust me."

She did the other side, her wet fingers rubbing over my clit, not intentionally, but it still sent a wave of heat through me. I ached, yearning to be touched or to touch myself. I knew my lips must be swollen—they felt huge, and so did my clit. I wondered if she could tell how wet I was, even with all the water running down between my legs.

"There!" She cocked her head and looked at her handiwork. "Lovely. You have nice big, puffy inner lips, Veronica. And your clit stands right out. It's very pretty."

I felt my cheeks burning. "Mrs. B..."

"It's true." She smiled, standing and rinsing the razor in the sink. "It's unusual... you should be proud of it."

I didn't know what to say. I put my legs down, closing my thighs. My pussy was wet from the shave, but it was also slick with excitement and when I squeezed my legs together, it made me feel faint. Things felt very different down there—vulnerable and exposed. I reached my hand down tentatively and gasped at how incredibly smooth my skin was now.

"Isn't that great?" Her eyes were bright. "I love how soft it is. Here, let's get you rinsed off. The fastest way is in the shower."

She had me stand at the back of the tub as she unhooked the showerhead and adjusted the water temperature. "Is that too hot?" She touched the spray to my feet.

I shook my head. "No."

Mrs. B knelt by the side of the tub, moving the water over my thighs and up to my pussy. "Open up." She looked up at me. "Use your fingers. Just spread your lips open."

Feeling the water running over my smooth, exposed labia was one thing, but having it spraying directly on my clit made me actually moan out loud with the pleasure of it.

"Here, let's try this." Mrs. B turned a knob on the shower massage. "That shaving cream can be irritating if it gets left on your skin. Want to make sure we get it all."

The water pulsed now, and she aimed it right between my legs. I could barely keep my eyes open, it felt so good! My knees wanted to buckle, but I held my pussy lips open for the hot throb of the water moving back and forth over my clit.

"Oh please, Mrs. B!" I pleaded, my head going back, my eyes closing fully now. The water got closer and closer to my pussy, the throb faster, harder, and I moaned, my head going from side to side. I couldn't stand it—it felt too good!

"Oh God," I whispered, feeling my climax beginning. I saw her watching me, her eyes bright, and felt ashamed to be doing this here in front of her, but I couldn't stop it. I shuddered and bucked my hips and moaned and bit my lip to try to keep from screaming as I came and came. Waves of pleasure rolled through my body, undulating my belly and hips toward the hot flow of the water between my legs.

"Good," she murmured, easing the pulse of the water back down my thighs. I felt her hand brush over my mound, touching me there, cupping me. It felt so good I thought I would die. "I think we got it all. Ready to get your suit on?"

I whimpered, opening my eyes to her as she shut off the water and grabbed another towel out of the linen closet. Stepping out of the tub, I took it from her, rubbing myself dry, my whole body flushed and filled with the heat of my orgasm. I glanced shyly over at her as she watched me, wondering if she knew, if she could tell?

"Here you go." She handed me the orange bikini bottoms. "Let's see how they look now." I slid them on, smoothing the straps over my hips and looking into the mirror. There wasn't a wisp of hair to be found peeking around it.

"Thanks." I smiled at her.

"My pleasure." She folded up the towel on the counter and put it in the sink. "Ready for that swim?"

"In a minute." I looked down at the floor. "I have to pee. I'll meet you out there."

"Okay." She turned and opened the door.

I collapsed onto the toilet seat when she went out, panting and flushed. I couldn't believe what had just happened, and yet Mrs. B acted like it was nothing—nothing at all! I cupped the triangle of orange material between my legs, feeling the gentle throb there still. My pussy felt different, new somehow—and so did I.

Chapter Five

They were all playing in the surf when I stepped outside into a wall of heat. It actually smelled and tasted like rain, although there wasn't a cloud in the sky. The humidity was like that down here, I'd discovered, and it seemed to force beads of sweat to the surface of my skin the minute I walked out of the air-conditioning.

Mrs. B saw me, waved, and I waved back. The white hot sand burned my feet, and I noticed how different everything felt between my legs now that I was shaved. I felt my swollen pussy lips rubbing together as I walked, constantly massaging my clit.

Janie and Henry took turns being tossed into the rolling waves by Doc, squealing and screeching as he hurled them out into the water. His arms were strong ropes of muscle, I noticed, working hard as he hefted them around. They weren't lightweights anymore. They came up sputtering and laughing, although it looked dangerous to me—but what did I know?

I was grateful when my feet greeted the wet sand and then the water's edge. Mrs. B looked over at me, shading her eyes against the sun. Her long blonde hair was pulled back into a ponytail and I remembered I didn't bring a Scrunchie.

"Hey, that's *your* bathing suit, Mom!" Janie wiped salt water out of her eyes.

"Yep," Mrs. B agreed as I began to wade out. "Veronica's borrowing it."

I saw Doc's gaze moving over me, lingering between my legs. It tingled there, as if his eyes were actually touching me. "Looks great, Ronnie."

"Thanks." I waded a little further out, wanting to bury myself in the water even though part of me liked the way he looked at me. I had to go by him to sink further in, and I swear I felt his eyes on my back. I was all too aware, except for two sets of string, I looked completely naked from behind.

I sank to my knees, pushing off the sandy bottom and skimming forward into the cool water. I went under for a moment to get my hair wet, slicking it back from my face as I came up near Mrs. B, where I could stand with the water up to my shoulders.

"Let's play Marco Polo!" Henry exclaimed, watching his father toss his sister into the water. She squealed and then held her nose, scrunching her face up as she went under.

"Yeah!" Janie burst up a moment later, obviously having heard her brother's remark before she went down. She rubbed water out of her eyes. "We have enough people! Let's play Marco Polo!"

"You're it, then, Henry," I called.

He closed his eyes and started counting to ten. We all moved away from him. Janie brushed past me, giggling, her wet blonde ponytail hanging to the middle of her back.

"Marco!" He did a blind-man walk forward, his hands out in front of him.

There was a chorus of "Polo's," and he struggled forward toward the voices. He was closest to me, his fingertips reaching out, and I tried to move back, but Janie clutched my hips and giggled as she hid behind me, making it impossible.

"I got you!" Henry opened his eyes when his fingers brushed my arm.

"That was a short one!" Mrs. B laughed.

"Janie's fault," I grumbled, turning and sticking my tongue out at her. "I'm coming for you, little girl! You better watch it!"

She squealed and moved away from me toward her mother as I closed my eyes and started to count to ten. I realized it was going to be a lot harder to play this in the ocean, with the sound of the waves crashing in on the shore, than it was in the glass surface of a pool.

I reached my hands out and strained to hear something as I counted. There was Janie, giggling, to my left. I turned toward the sound, rushing forward, trying to catch her, but came up empty.

"Ten... Marco!" I called, and I heard them all say "Polo!" Janie and her mom were to my left and so was Doc, but Henry was somewhere off to my right. Playing the odds, I lunged left and Janie squealed and splashed as she swam away.

"Marco!" I took a few more steps forward. Janie responded off to my right now, and so did Henry. Mrs. B was somewhere behind me, but I didn't hear Doc at all. I came to the slow realization he must be under water.

"Marco!" I said again, hearing the same responses, except this time Doc's "Polo" was right in front of me, his voice low. I reached a hand forward in the water and felt the smooth, hard planes of his stomach just above the elastic band of his suit. Gasping, I opened my eyes and saw him standing there, looking at me and smiling.

"Got me." He winked, his voice still low.

"Daddy, you're it!" Janie jumped up and down in the water.

We all moved away from him as he started counting. Janie still hid behind her mother, and Henry moved more toward shore. When Doc called "Marco!" I was still the closest one, and he followed my voice.

I went under for a moment, kicking hard and swimming the opposite direction past him. I heard him say a muffled "Marco!" again, but I kept swimming. Gasping as I came up, he said it again and I had to answer. He was inches away from Janie and Mrs. B, but when I said "Polo," he turned toward the sound of my voice.

I could look at him without him seeing me as he walked toward me, his dark, wet hair curling, the tanned skin of his chest and belly and arms beaded with water. I realized, if I could watch him, unnoticed, then he could have been watching me, too. That thought made my breath catch. He moved closer and closer, edging my way, and his body blocked out the sight of Mrs. B and Janie behind him.

"Marco!"

"Polo," I whispered.

His head turned toward me and he grinned, lunging at me just as I pushed off from the bottom, trying to swim away. We both went under for a moment, and he had me by my thigh, gripping his way up to my hips, his big body twisting against mine under the water. For a moment, I was beneath him, in his arms, pressed against him, and I felt something hard against my leg. I didn't realize, until his fingers brushed over my breast, sending shivers through me, what it was.

I came up gasping and so did he. We were out deeper now, and I had to stand on my tiptoes to stay up. He was under the water to his shoulders, his face inches from mine.

"You got me," I whispered, licking my lips and sliding my thigh against his. His eyes widened and then

I felt his fingers gripping my hips, his knee sliding up the inside of my thighs, dangerously high, until I heard Henry calling, "Ronnie's IT!"

I smiled as I turned away from him and started swimming back. He followed. We played a few more rounds, but then the kids got bored and wanted to go work on their "sand village."

We three "adults" spread out a couple blankets and laid out in the sun. Mrs. B was next to me and Doc had his own blanket on the other side of her. I looked over at Mrs. B. She was on her back, her arm thrown over her eyes. I couldn't help watching her breasts rise and fall with her breath, full and fleshy under the white bikini top. I called up the memory of what she looked like laying there topless.

Doc moved up on his elbow, facing me, and when I met his eyes, he smiled. I felt him watching, his gaze moving over me like a heat. I stretched, arching my back, and saw his eyes widen and then darken, his smile fading as he watched me roll to my side and then over onto my belly, adjusting my straps.

My skin and hair were still wet from the swim, and the heat of the sun felt good. I opened my legs a little bit, lifting my hips, knowing that my bare ass rose up in the air as I did. Through half-closed eyes, I watched him watch me, a lazy smile on my face. I couldn't help glancing down at his crotch, and even in the loose material of the suit, I he was hard. I licked my lips, remembering the length of him, how his hand moved up and down the shaft.

My now-bare pussy tingled with feeling, and I wished I was alone so I could touch it. I fantasized about his hand there, those big fingers spreading me open. I glanced down at his suit again and saw him shifting, moving things around, and wondered what it would feel like in my hand…my mouth…inside of me. My pussy ached at the thought.

I was totally lost in my fantasy when a stream of cold water splashed over my back, making me scream and kneel up. Henry laughed and ran, trailing a blue bucket behind him.

"Ooooo you're going to get it!" I stood up and took off after him.

I caught up with him at the shoreline, grabbing his swimming trunks. He squealed and apologized, laughing still. I tackled him, straddling and tickling him. He howled, twisting.

"Stop, stop! I'm sorry!" He begged, gasping. Janie watched, grinning.

"Henry, you shouldn't have done that." Doc stood behind me and I shaded my eyes as I looked up at him. He grinned, too. "As irresistible as the target may have seemed."

"Very funny." I stood up.

Henry still giggled as he stood, too. "Hop on pop!" He tackled his father.

Doc groaned, catching him with one arm. Janie squealed, running towards him, and he braced himself for her, mock-falling back onto the sand when she hit him in the chest. He laid sprawled in the sand while the kids crawled over him, trying to tickle him.

"You know I'm not ticklish." He looked up at me as I walked by. "But I bet Ronnie is."

"Hey!" He had hold of my ankle and I gasped, trying to shake him loose. "Oh, no, you don't!"

"Hop on babysitter!" Doc called, and the kids screeched, jumping up to tackle me. I couldn't get away with the hold he had on my ankle, and I tumbled to the sand as Henry and Janie tickled my ribs, making me laugh.

"Stop!" I gasped, rolling away from them, but Doc still had my ankle, and now his other hand was on my calf, moving up.

"I'll hold her!" Doc grabbed my hip and used it as leverage to roll me onto my back. I was helpless, laughing as Henry and Janie dug their little fingers into my ribs. "You tickle her."

My eyes widened as Doc climbed on top of me, straddling me. He grabbed my arms, pinning them above my head. My eyes met his, shocked and excited, and he saw it, putting his mouth next to my ear, the heat of his breath making me tremble.

"Got you," he whispered, moving his hips just a little, letting me feel how hard he was, the length of him pressed right there between my lips. My clit felt like it was pulsing against the head of his cock.

"Stop, stop, stop!" I begged as the kids' fingers found their way under my arms, making me twist and squeal underneath him. I couldn't stop laughing, and still the feel of his erection between my legs made my pussy throb and my head pound.

"Okay, okay!" He sat up a little, looking into my eyes. "I think the babysitter's had enough."

I shook my head and mouthed the word, "No," meeting Doc's eyes and moving my hips up just a little bit with the tiniest, almost imperceptible rock. He pressed into me, squeezing my wrists once, hard, before letting me go.

Henry took his father at his word and tackled Janie then, trying to tickle her, and they rolled and kicked in the sand. Doc moved off me and headed for the water, and I knew why—because he was hard as a rock. That thought left me breathless. I stood, brushing sand off of me. Henry got bored and went back to digging a "moat" around his "castle." Janie joined him after a breathless minute.

"Carrie!" Doc waved toward shore. I saw Mrs. B sit up, shading her eyes. "Come swim with me!"

I wiped sand off my arms while I watched her wade into the water, swimming out to where he was standing. He grabbed her, twirling her around, making her squeal, and I watched them, feeling something hard and tight in the pit of my stomach.

I went and got one of the floats from the side of the house, climbing onto it and paddling through the waves. I lay on my belly, letting the water rock me up and down as I watched them playing together. They were a good ways off from me, splashing and laughing.

I closed my eyes and drifted, spreading my thighs and letting my feet dangle in the water, hugging the float to my body. The water rocked me a little closer, close enough I could hear them.

"No one will know," Doc said, and I opened one eye, seeing Mrs. B with her arms around his neck. They were shoulder-deep in the water. "Please, baby."

"Doc," she admonished, glancing toward shore, and then over at me. I made my eyes into slits, hoping to look as if I were sleeping. I knew what he wanted, because I wanted it, too. My pussy was aching, my clit a humming little swell between my thighs.

I saw his thumbs moving over her nipples through her white bikini top, making her gasp. He kept that up as he kissed her. I was close enough now I could see his tongue slipping into her mouth. I licked my lips, swallowing hard, the heat of the sun on my back nothing compared to the fire burning between my legs.

I saw Mrs. B glance over at the kids and then back at me. "What about Veronica?"

"She's not paying attention." Doc glanced over at me, too. "Please, Carrie? God, I can't stand it."

Mrs. B's hand moved under the water, and I realized she must have his cock in it. That thought made my clit beg to be touched, and I slipped a hand slowly underneath me, edging under the tiny triangle of my suit.

"That's it, baby!" Doc moaned, and I saw him bucking against her. "God, I want to fuck you."

My fingers eased between my swollen lips, rubbing at my clit as I watched her straddle him, wrapping her legs around his waist. I couldn't see anything with the water rushing around them, but I knew he was sliding his cock up inside of her from the way their eyes closed, the way they moved together, a little different rhythm from the waves that rocked me up and down on the float.

She wrapped herself around him, biting his shoulder, digging her nails into his back. He turned with her in his arms, so her back was to me, and I saw his face, his eyes closed as he fucked her. My clit asked to be rubbed harder, faster, and I did. I couldn't help it. I watched them openly now, working my hand under my tummy, between my legs, feeling that familiar tug and swell.

"I'm gonna come!" He pulled her hard into him, and I came, too, quivering and gasping, trying not to make any noise at all as a white, pulsing heat filled my body. I imagined his cum shooting up inside of *me*, the feel of his cock throbbing as he came, and when I opened my eyes I saw him looking at me. He kissed Mrs. B's shoulder, her neck, but his eyes were on mine and he smiled.

"Thank you, baby," he murmured, nuzzling her. I bit my lip, shivering, sliding my hand out from between my legs, making sure he saw me. His eyes widened as I lifted my fingers to my mouth, sucking and licking them as he watched.

Chapter Six

I was supposed to be taking Janie and Henry shopping with Mrs. B. That was the plan, mostly because Mr. and Mrs. B had a big party to go to that night and she didn't have anything to wear, she said. The kids got bored quick, though, and I didn't blame them. There were only so many Louis Vuitton purses and Gucci scarves an eight year old could stand to look at before getting whiny.

Frankly, I was starting to get whiny, myself, even after we took a distracting trip through the Disney Store for an hour or so. Mrs. B didn't seem anywhere near ready to quit.

It wasn't until we stopped for lunch that we all got saved.

"Oh my God, Maureen Holmes! Is that you?" Mrs. B stood up and I watched her kiss the air next to the cheek of a woman with short, stylish dark hair who had two children trailing behind her. They looked a little younger than Janie and Henry. There was also a girl about my age with a blonde ponytail holding their hands.

Small world—they were acquaintances of the Baumgartners from back home, and Janie and Henry jumped at the chance to have playmates their own age again. The older women chatted, and me and the blonde—her name was Gretchen and she was the Holmes' *au pair*, she told me—wrangled the kids.

As Gretchen and I talked, I realized that she actually got paid for doing for the Holmes' what I was doing for the Baumgartners for free. When it was time to go, all four of the kids had a meltdown, and we stood around with the eyes of restaurant patrons on us, wondering what to do.

"Why don't I take them all back to the house?" Gretchen suggested, smiling at Mrs. Holmes. "You can come pick them up later, Mrs. Baumgartner. I'm sure the kids would love to play together a while longer, and it would give you two a chance to catch up some more."

And just like that, the *au pair* saved the day. The two women looked at her like she was wearing tights and cape with a big "S" on the back.

"Do you want to just go back to the house, Veronica?" Mrs. B asked me. "I'm sure Gretchen can handle the kids."

And that's how I ended up with the whole afternoon to myself. I walked home, since it was only half a mile, enjoying the sunshine. I went for a swim when I got back, then took a shower and painted my toenails. I called my sister, Amy, and my best friend, Jenny, back home. Then I curled up with a book on my bed and fell asleep and didn't wake up until someone came in downstairs.

It was Doc. He called up to see if anyone was home, but I was still half-asleep and I didn't answer. Really, it was just that I was still too flushed and embarrassed to reply. I'd been dreaming about Mrs. B lying on a towel on the beach. I was straddling her waist and pouring oil onto her breasts and rubbing it in. She was moaning and saying, "More on the nipples, Veronica. In circles."

I almost fell back asleep, still imagining what it would feel like to run my slick hands over Mrs. B's heavy breasts, when I heard moaning from downstairs. For a moment, I was caught in that liminal space between sleep and consciousness and thought it must be my dream.

Then I heard it again, a woman moaning, saying, "Fuck me! Harder! That's it!"

I sat up in bed, tilting my head and listening. Was Mrs. B home? Where were the kids? Remembering the other night, when I stood outside of the Baumgartners' room and watched Doc and Mrs. B together, I crept quietly down the hallway. The moaning was louder, now, and I could also hear music.

Then Doc's voice, "Oooo yeah, baby."

I sat on the first step, my breath held, trying to puzzle out what I was hearing. I slid quietly down a step, and then one more, looking through the banister. From my vantage point, I saw the television, a huge widescreen, flat-panel that made the already formidable Shrek seem a life-size ten feet tall. Shrek wasn't on it, though—rather, a dark-haired girl in pigtails bent over the arm of a big, comfy chair, was being fucked from behind by an older man with an enormous cock.

And I had thought Doc's was big...

I made an immediate direct comparison, because Doc leaned back on the sofa, his jeans pushed down his hips. His cock was hard, and he gripped and pumped it while he watched what was happening on the screen.

I stared, unable to look away as the girl put her leg up over the chair, giving the camera a better view. My exposure to porn had pretty much been limited to a few Internet pop-ups, so this was all new to me. I looked at the girl's face—she looked young, probably my age, and she had a red lollipop she was sucking and licking on.

Her pussy was shaved completely, I noticed, and it glistened as his cock slammed into her. I felt the throb of my own shaved pussy when I squeezed my legs together. Doc pumped a little faster now, his other hand reaching down and cupping his balls. I bit my lip, seeing his eyes half-closed, the look of pleasure on his face.

My breath came faster as I unbuttoned my cut-offs, sliding the zipper down the teeth a notch at a time, afraid he might hear, even over the moaning and grunting on the television. As I watched, the cock which had been plunging into her slid out, pulsing and thick with her wetness. It was bigger than Doc's but it reminded me of him, and my eyes flicked to his hand shuttling up and down the length.

"Put that big dick in my little pussy, Mr. Smith!" The girls voice was high and breathy. She reached back and spread herself open, the lollipop still in her hand.

"Yeahhhhhh!" The guy on the screen groaned as he shoved his cock back inside of her. "God, you've got such a tight little hole, baby girl."

From the sofa, Doc groaned, too, his hand slowing on his cock, squeezing the tip hard. The girl's pigtails bounced with every thrust, and she moaned and rocked. She reached her lollipop between her legs and the camera zoomed in on her bare slit as she rubbed it over and over her clit. I stared, feeling the pulse of my own clit.

I wedged my hand down into my cutoffs, fingers probing the moist heat of my pussy, so sensitive now that it was bald and exposed. Doc pumped his cock again, his hand gripping the top, moving the loose skin over the head. I saw the tip of it was a little wet and wondered what it tasted like.

Rubbing my clit was difficult like this because the seam of my cutoffs rode against my hand when I moved. I shifted, frustrated, as I watched Doc's hand slip up under his shirt. He tweaked his nipple, groaning and thrusting upward.

The girl sucked her lollipop again, arching her back and looking over her shoulder at the older man fucking her. She made a little pout with her lips and asked in that same breathy, high voice, "Do you like fucking the babysitter, Mr. Smith?"

Doc groaned out loud, and I saw him squeeze the tip of his cock again until it turned bright red. His hips moved, his head back and his eyes closed. "He loves fucking the babysitter, sweetheart!" I heard Doc murmur, opening his eyes again halfway.

He used his palm to rub the wet head of his cock. I flushed, wondering if he was thinking about me. The girl on the screen looked a little like me—the dark hair and eyes, the slender body and small breasts. The thought made me desperate to touch myself. I tried rubbing the seam of my jeans over my clit, but it was just a tease. I needed more stimulation. I stood on the step, balancing as I slid my cutoffs and panties off.

My fingers slid through the slippery, wet folds of flesh of my pussy, so soft and smooth. I could open my legs now, and I did, shifting to lean back against the wall at a better angle to see both Doc and the screen. I spread and pulled on my lips as I watched the babysitter who looked a little like me get fucked by that great big cock.

The girl was on top of him now, a jerky transition as she sat on his cock, facing the camera, her movements uncoordinated and unsure. He grabbed her hips, putting her legs up, and gripped her ass, fucking her from underneath. His motion was fluid, fast and hard, making her moan, her tiny breasts bouncing up and down.

"Yeah!" Doc moaned at the television, his hand speeding up. "Fuck her good."

I slipped my fingers inside of my pussy, staring at Doc's stiff cock. It was swollen and red, and although it paled in comparison to the enormous thing on the screen, it was real flesh, engorged with blood, being pumped just ten feet from me. I could hear the sound of it, the slap and shuffle of his hand from base to tip.

I teased my clit with my fingers, rubbing it in circles. I was already so wet I could feel my juices slipping down the crack of my ass. That was one thing about being shaved—there was nothing there to impede the flow. My panties were wet all the time now.

"Mr. Smith, what are you doing!" the pigtailed girl gasped. I watched as he turned her over, his wet fingers probing her asshole. I stared, stunned, open mouthed.

"Yeahhhh," Doc moaned, moving his hips lower on the sofa. "Fuck that tight little asshole." Shocked, I stared at the screen where that enormous cock was easing into a place it never should have even thought about going.

Horrified, I didn't think, I just reacted—I gasped out loud.

Doc turned his head toward the stairs, and I knew he could see me through the banister, my shorts off, my legs spread. I sat for a moment, paralyzed, and so did he, our eyes locking.

Then, I grabbed my cutoffs and ran upstairs to my room. I heard him following me and I slammed my door, mortified, burying my face in my pillow.

"Ronnie?" He opened my door without knocking. "I didn't know you were here."

"Go away!" I moaned into my pillow. I hadn't even had time to put my shorts back on.

"It's okay," he said, his voice reassuring. "You don't have to be embarrassed."

"Go away," I moaned again, shaking my head.

"You're beautiful, Ronnie." I turned my face a little, listening. "Did it feel good?" he asked after a moment. "Touching yourself like that?"

My pussy was still wet and aching to be touched. "Yes," I admitted.

"It feels good when I do it, too," he said. "It's normal, you know. Totally natural."

I nodded, hugging my pillow. "I know."

He didn't say anything for a moment, but I heard a sound that had become familiar to me—his hand slipping up and down the length of his cock.

I rolled over, and sure enough, he was standing there in my doorway, his jeans down over his hips, stiff cock in his hand.

"Doc..." I lifted my eyes to his. If I'd thought he was looking at me with lust the other day on the beach...suffice it to say that now I knew what real lust looked like. His eyes darkened with it as they moved over my body, focusing between my legs.

"It feels good," he murmured, and I shifted my gaze back down to his hand as it moved faster. "Don't you want to keep touching yourself?"

I made a noise, half moan, half whimper, nodding.

"Spread your legs for me, Ronnie." He squeezed the head again. "Please?"

I hesitated, seeing his eyes focused between my thighs, the look in them making me feel faint. He looked like he could eat me alive.

"Go ahead," he said, and I heard his breath coming faster. Mine was, too. "I won't touch you or do anything, I promise. I just want to see you."

I opened for him, my knees up and falling to the side. He groaned, his hand moving rapidly.

"You're so fucking beautiful," he whispered, his face almost pained as he looked at me. "Will you pull up your shirt and let me see all of you?"

I swallowed, nodding, squirming under his gaze as I slipped my t-shirt off and undid the front hook on my bra, letting it fall open. I leaned back on my elbows now, completely nude.

He let out a slow breath through pursed lips, shaking his head. "Do you know how much I want you?"

I shook my head, blushing, feeling how much as he looked at me, seeing it in the red throbbing of the cock in his hand.

"If you don't mind, I'm going to keep doing this," he murmured, pumping, that slick sound filling the room. "Mostly because you're so fucking beautiful I can't stop..."

I stared, my mouth a little open, my eyes half-closed, aching all over.

"But what I really want is to see you touch yourself," he whispered, his eyes between my legs. "I want to see you come. Would you do that for me?"

I blushed, feeling a heat creeping over my cheeks and my chest, but I slipped my hand between my thighs. He nodded his encouragement, leaning against the door frame and groaning when I spread my lips open with my fingers, looking for my clit.

His reaction made me bolder and I used both hands, pulling my lips apart, showing him. He made a noise in his throat, his hand flying up and down his shaft now. I used my fingers to rub my clit, moaning a little as I circled it faster and faster. I was so excited now, I was dripping wet.

"Good girl," he breathed, and I watched him, too, the sound of our labored breathing filling the room. He moved a little further into the doorway, his eyes burning between my thighs.

"Oh, Doc," I moaned, using my palm to rub my nipple, making it hard, sending shivers through me. It felt so good I could barely breathe.

"Yes," he murmured, taking a few more steps toward my bed, looking down at me. His hand was a blur over his shaft, but I could still see the red tip, wet with pre-cum.

"Oh, God," I gasped, rocking my hips, arching, pulling at my nipples and twisting them as I played with my clit. "My pussy feels so good."

He groaned, standing beside the bed now. I could have reached out and touched his cock, and I wanted to, but didn't dare. I looked up at him and saw he was staring at my fingers, moving back and forth in my wetness, now, teasing my clit toward release.

"Doc, I'm close," I whispered, feeling that sweet ache reaching a delicious peak, the hot friction of my fingers driving me upward fast. He nodded, squeezing the head of his cock again, and this time I could see it actually throbbing between his fingers, the tip leaking a clear, thick fluid.

"Come on," he growled, and he started stroking again, aiming his cock toward where my fingers were massaging my pussy, fast and furious now. I was breathless and gasping, and I bit my lip to keep from crying out as the first wave of my orgasm washed over me.

"Ohhhh now," I moaned, closing my eyes, my whole body shuddering with hot, delicious spasms of pleasure. I felt the first spurt of his cum before I saw it, like fire across my belly. I gasped and moaned, looking down at the thick white rope of cum, like an arrow pointing its way toward my throbbing pussy.

I watched, still quivering, as he groaned and pumped his cock through his fist, shooting more hot fluid over my trembling belly. When he was spent, he leaned his hand against the wall, panting, resting his forehead on his arm.

"That felt so good," I murmured, and he smiled when he looked at me, nodding. His eyes were still glazed and I wondered if I looked like that, too.

We both jumped at the sound of the door downstairs and Mrs. B's voice calling up, "Doc?"

"Fuck," he swore, hauling his jeans up and I heard Janie and Henry down there too, arguing about something.

He looked back at me from the doorway. "You really are beautiful."

I sighed when he shut the door, looking down at the pool of cum accumulating in my navel. Smiling, I dipped a finger into it, bringing it to my mouth. It was a sharp taste, a little acrid, but I sucked it off my finger anyway, remembering how he looked as he came all over my tummy.

Chapter Seven

"Veronica, can I get your opinion about something?" Mrs. B poked her head around the door to find me curled up on my bed.

"Sure." I put down my book. "What's up?"

They were getting ready to go out, and Henry and Janie were already asleep. They'd obviously worn themselves out playing with the Holmes' kids. Henry actually nodded off over his spaghetti, and Doc kept taking bets on whether or not his nose would end up in it. I won—I said he wouldn't end up with his face in the plate—although a couple times, I thought for sure he was a goner. Doc paid up, though—five bucks.

"I need a girl's eye." Mrs. B motioned for me to follow her. "Doc's no help with these things."

I trailed after her into their room, a little hesitant, not knowing if Doc was up here. I heard the TV on downstairs, though, and I thought he was probably down there. Mrs. B had two dresses hung over the door and she was wearing a third, a long, brown, satin halter dress. She turned to take the other two dresses down and tossed them next to me on the bed.

"Ok, there's this one." She went over to the mirror and turned, first left, then right. "What do you think?"

I shrugged. "It seems a little formal. What kind of party is this?"

"This dress is a Nicole Miller," she added, as if that might mean something to me. I found myself much more interested in who was in the dress than who'd designed it. "Oh, it's a fancy kind of party. All the men in suits sort of thing."

I watched her turn in the dress, the lush brown satin moving over her hips like it was part of her. She smoothed it like liquid over her belly and reached up to lift her breasts. Her hands on them gave me a start, even through the material, and I couldn't help but remember her cupping and tweaking them, her hair falling back and brushing Doc's chest as she rocked against his mouth. Her hands took the weight of them, lifting and pushing them together in the fabric as I watched, feeling that slow heat spreading through me.

She winked at me in the mirror. "Gonna need the push-up bra, no matter what we decide."

"It's beautiful." I reached out to finger the material as she came to stand beside me to look at the other dresses. There was a long slit up the side and my fingers touched the softness of her thigh as I rubbed the satin. She gave me a warm smile, her eyes seeming to know something, and my breath caught and my belly clenched.

"Let's try this one." She pulled out a black silk dress, another halter with velvet trim. I watched as she untied the brown satin halter behind her neck, sliding the dress down her hips. Her breasts swayed as she stepped out of it, and the dress pulled her black panties down a little. She adjusted them, her fingers snapping the elastic, before she stepped into the black dress, pulling it up tight and holding the ties around her neck.

"What about this one?" She turned again so I could see. It shimmered on her body like it was made of liquid. "It's a Vera Wang."

"I love it," I replied, not caring at all who Vera Wang was as I saw this one slit up to mid-thigh on both sides as she walked. "It really shows off your tan."

She smiled, dropping the halter and coming toward me topless, working the dress down her hips. Her brown nipples were stiff, probably from cold, but she was so close I could see the skin pursed around them. I couldn't help but remember Doc's hands on them, her own hands on them, and then I found myself imagining my hands on them. What would they feel like, the weight of them, cupped in my palms? I looked down at the carpet, feeling a little breathless.

Mrs. B tossed the black silk onto the bed. "See, if I had tan lines, none of these dresses would work very well, would they?"

"Good point," I agreed as she lifted the last dress, a raspberry red chiffon slip dress with spaghetti straps. This one went on like a second skin. The bodice was crossed and pleated, making her breasts appear even larger, and the plunging neckline gave a good view of the swell of her cleavage.

"Zip me?" She backed up until she was pressed between my thighs. I was wearing shorts and I couldn't tell which was softer, the material rubbing against my legs or her skin. I grasped the little zipper and it went up like I was sealing her in.

"This one?" She twirled a little, the chiffon skirt showing a generous amount of her long, brown legs when she did. "It's a Susana Monaco. Oh, but wait!" Mrs. B moved the black and brown pile of satin and silk and pulled out a long chiffon scarf, the same color as the dress. She wrapped it once around her neck, letting the ends hang down to her hips in front and back.

"Ohhh," I breathed, fascinated by the way little stray blonde hairs curled at the nape of her neck and around her face with her hair up, how the scarf just drew more attention to it. "That's the one. Perfect."

She smiled, looking pleased, and turned back to the mirror. "That's what I thought, but it's good to get another woman's opinion."

I didn't know why, but Mrs. B calling me a woman made me feel warm and tingly. She dug through the closet and found a pair of strappy shoes with incredibly high stiletto heels. They looked scary-high to me. She put each foot up on the vanity table chair to do the straps, the muscles in her slim calves flexing, and then walked around in them like a pro.

"Now I just have to find a bra." She went over and rummaged through her drawers. "Ah, here we are." She held a black one up. "Here, can you unzip me, Veronica?"

I watched as the smooth, tawny skin of her back was revealed when the zipper parted. I brushed my fingers over her spine as I unzipped her, trying to make it seem accidental. I just had to touch her. When I had it all the way down, I saw the lace top of her black panties and the two dimples just above them. She lifted her breasts into the bra cups and reached around to do the hooks. Her fingernails were their usual red and almost matched the dress.

"There." She adjusted. "Zipper?"

I closed it back up, feeling the slight resistance as the material stretched around her flesh. When she turned around, I gasped. The bra pressed her breasts up high—firm golden orbs nestled together in the red pleated fabric.

She laughed and exclaimed, "I know! Thank you, Victoria's Secret!"

"Carrie?" Doc called up the stairs. "Almost?"

"Almost!" She grabbed the hangers for the other two dresses and started to put them back.

"Let me do that," I offered, holding my hands out for them. She gave the hangers to me with a smile, leaning in to kiss my cheek. I knew I would have a lipstick mark there.

"You're such a sweetheart," she murmured against my ear and the smell of her perfume made me heady. She paused at the door, looking back at me. "We won't be too late. Midnight or so."

"Okay." I swallowed as I stared at her curves and tried not to be too obvious. She seemed to know it, though. I could tell by the little smile that played on her lips, the way her eyes seemed brighter.

"Have a good night," she said as I started putting the black dress back on a hanger.

"You too," I replied as she went out the door and started down the hall. "Oh, Mrs. B..." She turned to look at me over her shoulder, her hand on the railing, as I peeked out the door. To me, she looked like a picture from a magazine and it took my breath away. "You really look beautiful," I gushed, feeling my face flush.

Her smile was pure warmth. "Thank you."

I heard Doc whistle when she got downstairs and wondered what it would be like to have someone react to me like that. Then I remembered how he stood over me, pumping his cock in his fist as he looked between my legs. Did he think I was beautiful? He had said so... I heard the sound of Doc's keys and the door close downstairs as I gathered the dresses and hung them back up in the closet with a sigh.

Mrs. B left her bras hanging out of her drawers and I started putting them back in, straightening. That's when I saw it, although at first, I couldn't believe what I was seeing. I just stared into her drawer, not touching it, as if it might burn me. It was an enormous black vibrator tangled in one of her pink bras.

Just looking at it made me feel faint, and I stood there imagining Mrs. B sliding it into her slick, shaved pussy. Did Doc watch her? Did she play by herself? I'd never used a dildo or a vibrator before, although I'd seen one (my mother had one hidden away in her drawers, too) and I'd heard a lot about them from my best friend, Jenny, who owned three and kept telling me I *had* to try one.

I took it out of the drawer, feeling the weight of it in my hand. It was huge, much bigger than any cock I'd ever seen, and it was shaped just like a cock, with the bulbous tip and veined shaft. I turned the red dial on the bottom and it buzzed gently, making me jump. Curious, I turned it further, and the buzzing got louder, stronger, the sound filling the room. I turned it off quickly, as if someone might hear, looking around and feeling guilty.

Still, my shorts felt damp now and my pussy had gone from tingle to throb. I reached my hand down, cupping myself through my shorts and rubbing, staring at the cock in my hand. What would it feel like? I bit my lip, rubbing a little faster and glancing back at the bed. It was so tempting... and so naughty.

"To hell with it!" I crawled onto the bed and took the big black cock with me. Rolling over to my back, I slid my shorts down over my hips. My panties were damp, all right, the crotch wet to the touch. Watching Mrs. B change had me more turned-on than I had even realized. I grabbed the vibrator, turning the dial on so it buzzed gently and slid the tip lightly over my panties.

"Oh my God," I whispered as it hummed against my clit. I shivered, gasping, pressing the big black head harder against the white cotton crotch. It made my pussy sing! I tugged my panties off, spreading my legs wide and slowly slipped the vibrating tip through my soft, wet flesh. I moaned, my nipples getting hard under my t-shirt as I rubbed the shaft up and down between my slit. I couldn't believe how good it felt!

Did Mrs. B lie in this bed and do this? I remembered the smell of her, the soft feel of her thighs between mine when I zipped her dress, the way her breasts moved and swayed when she bent over, revealing the rounded curves of her behind. Doc would come home and zip her out of that dress, I knew, and probably fuck her right here in this bed. And I would listen to them and touch myself and fantasize some more—I knew I would, I just couldn't help it.

The vibrator was slick with my juices now, and I lifted it to my mouth, sucking on the tip, imagining I was tasting Mrs. B on the tip of Doc's cock. I groaned, turning the dial up a little more and rubbing the black head back and forth over my clit again. God, that was good! Jenny wasn't kidding, I thought, my other hand creeping up under my shirt, tweaking my nipple. The sensation sent shockwaves through me and I felt like I was floating.

What did Mrs. B think about when she played with this? Did she fantasize about another man? A woman? I remembered how she looked at me and touched me the day she shaved my pussy, how her eyes had watched me while I came. Did she fantasize about me? That thought went through me like fire and I moaned, rubbing the vibrator faster between my legs.

Did she fuck herself with this hard, humming cock until her pussy squelched and her body convulsed on the bed as she came? I pulled my legs back a little, looking down between them as I slid the big head down toward the opening of my pussy. I could imagine Mrs. B between my legs, that look in her eyes. Would she fuck me with it? Would she slide it slowly in, like I was now, her eyes watching it sink deeper into my flesh?

"Ohhhh God," I whispered, feeling the vibration inside of me now, through my whole pelvis. I turned the dial up more, gasping and squirming on the bed. It felt huge inside, a thick, humming length filling me to bursting. I moved it, slow and easy, in and out of my pussy, listening to the soft, wet sounds it made.

I saw myself in the vanity mirror, my legs wide open, my t-shirt up, my nipples pointing toward the ceiling. I watched the enormous shaft disappear into my pussy about halfway and then reappear again, glistening in the lamplight. I fucked myself, imagining her fucking me, almost feeling her breath on my thighs, her hair brushing me, hearing her soft, encouraging moans.

"Mrs. B," I murmured, lost in the fantasy, still watching myself in the mirror with half-closed eyes. I remembered how Mrs. B talked to Doc in bed and I tried the words on for size, feeling myself flush even as I said them. "Oh yeah, fuck me, Mrs. B... fill my pussy with that big cock."

That's when I heard it—a small hiss or gasp? I was so involved I didn't stop, just slowed, listening. Was it the kids? Maybe I'd just imagined it and it was really just the buzz of the vibrator? I watched myself in the mirror and realized the door was open a little bit, just like it had been when I stood there and watched the Baumgartners.

I moved the vibrator deeper into my pussy, moaning a little, and catching a movement in the mirror out of the corner of my eye, a flash of red, and suddenly I just knew. I didn't know how I knew, I just did, and the jolt that went through me was both shocking and exciting. Mrs. B had come back and was watching me.

I tried not to let on I knew, still fucking myself with the vibrator, moaning a little louder for her benefit. I saw her out of the corner of my eye now, saw her cheek resting on the doorframe, her mouth a little open. I wouldn't let myself watch her for long, too afraid she would discover I knew, but I was fascinated by the movement I saw below the doorknob, that little flash of red, moving faster and faster.

I pulled the slick cock from my pussy, spreading my legs even wider, pulling them back to give her a full view as I slid the wet head up and down. I moaned whenever the buzzing tip brushed my clit, and I knew if I kept it there for more than a few seconds, I would come—and hard! I wanted it to last, so I teased my lips, inside and out, with the buzzing shaft and head, over and over.

"Fuck me, Mrs. B," I murmured, full to bursting with the knowledge she was watching me, sliding the black head back into the opening of my pussy, feeling it spread me wide. "Fuck me with that big, black dick."

I heard the little hiss again and knew she was hearing my words. That drove me on as I pushed it deeper into me, my hand moving faster and faster. I fucked myself hard now, my whole pelvis rocking with a delicious hum as I moaned and bucked my hips.

I thought I heard her breathing, just as fast as mine, and I let myself peek in the mirror, seeing the crack in the door was wider now. I saw her face, so flushed, her eyes half-closed, and I saw her dress pulled up and her hand slipped down into the crotch of the sheer black panties.

"God, I want you, Mrs. B," I moaned, feeling my clit moving closer to the edge with each tender throb, the buzz of the vibrator sending hot, electric sparks through my pussy.

"Oh, I want you, I want you," I whimpered, shoving the cock deep, closing my eyes and panting, working the dildo between my legs as fast and hard as I could.

That's when I felt her fingers brushing my thighs. At first I thought I must be imagining it, but when I opened my eyes, there she was, her breasts spilling over the top of her dress, her nipples playing peek-a-boo with the material as her hand worked between her legs.

"Ohhh," I moaned, feeling embarrassed and too close to coming to care.

"Shh," she whispered, shaking her head and taking the end of the vibrator in her hand, twisting it and moving it in my flesh.

"Oh God," I groaned, feeling her fucking me with the thick cock. "Yes, yes, please... oh, it feels so good!"

"Good girl," she whispered, fucking me with the slick length, turning it up as high it would go, making me groan and writhe and twist on the bed. "Come for me."

"Yes!" I lifted my hips in the air, off the bed toward her, bridging up, wanting more and more. Mrs. B groaned, seeing me splayed out like that, and I was so close I couldn't stand it.

That's when she sucked my clit into her mouth, sending me over the edge so fast I thought I was going to die quivering and trembling from the delicious throbbing wetness between my thighs.

I groaned when she slid the cock from my pussy and I came back down to earth, and to the bed, watching her lift it to her mouth and suck on the tip. I gasped as she lifted her dress further, pointing the wet cock down and sliding it under the elastic of her panties.

"Mrs. B," I whispered, watching her rubbing the length up and down, up and down, her eyes closed, her moans filling the room. I whispered, "Oh God. You're so beautiful," although I didn't know if she heard me. She was lost in the sensation, rocking against the buzzing cock rubbing over her pussy.

Then her eyes opened and met mine, her gaze moving down over my heaving chest, my taut nipples, my smooth, flat belly, to the slick wetness between my legs, still seeping with my juices. She groaned, putting one red-tipped finger against my clit, making me shiver, and then I watched as she came, her whole body flushing and shuddering with it.

"Fuck!" she whispered and let out a half-cry, half-groan, the cock lost somewhere between her legs. She gave me a dazed look as she slipped the vibrator out of her panties, her dress falling down to cover her.

"Mrs. B," I started, not sure what I was even going to try to say.

She shook her head, turning the vibrator off but pressing the head to my mouth. I gasped, but I opened my lips, slowly sucking and licking the tip, tasting her for the first time, our eyes meeting, the air between us charged like some electrical field. I took the vibrator from her, continuing to lick at it as she watched.

"I forgot my earrings." She adjusted her bra and her dress, going over to her dresser and opening a small box on top. I watched as she slipped her earrings on, feeling dazed and kind of floating.

I rolled onto my side and pulled my t-shirt down as far as I could. "I don't know what to say."

She glanced back at me and I could see her mouth was glistening with my juices, like she was wearing lip gloss. "We'll talk about it later, Veronica," she said, still breathless. "Good night."

With that, she was out the door and down the stairs and if I couldn't still taste her in my mouth, I might have thought that I dreamed it all.

Chapter Eight

"Some babysitter I am." I gave a little laugh, pulling my knees up to my chin and watching the sun set across the horizon. Mrs. B glanced away from her book, a paperback copy of *The Davinci Code* that I had loaned her, and smiled.

"I'm glad the kids found something else to do." She stretched on the lounge chair with a yawn.

They'd gotten in very late from their party, past two. I knew because I heard them laughing and trying to be quiet in the hallway as they fumbled their way to their room. Then came Mrs. B's moans and Doc's grunting followed by the rhythmic bang of the headboard against the wall and the squeak and shift of their bed.

I rolled around for a while trying to sleep but eventually couldn't help slipping my hand between my legs and rubbing myself until I was breathless and panting and shuddering all over with my orgasm as I listened to the sounds of them together.

"I just feel bad." I shrugged. "You brought me along to watch the kids, and they're spending all their time with the Holmes' au pair." Doc had taken Janie and Henry over to the Holmes' to spend the night.

Mrs. B set her book aside, reaching over and fingering a strand of my hair. "That's not all you're here for, you know." My belly seized when she said that and I looked at her, wondering if I understood what she really meant. "You're one of the family, really." She tucked a piece of hair behind my ear. "This was kind of like a gift for you, a thank you for everything you've done for us."

I was almost disappointed by her words, but I smiled, looking back out over the water. It had been a crazy-hot week and today was the worst. We hadn't even gone to lay out. Mrs. B's borrowed orange micro-bikini was still hanging in the bathroom.

Now, though, it had started to cool a little, although the air was so humid it was still like trying to breathe through a wet washcloth. The sun was sinking fast and spreading orange fire across the horizon.

"I've really...had a good time," I told her, still not looking her way. "It's been...a very exciting week."

"I'm glad." Mrs. B's fingers moved in my hair, caressing me just behind the ear, sending shivers through me.

Sometimes I just didn't know what to say or how to act around them. We never talked about the things that happened, although there was always some undercurrent of communication going on, lower than our words, like our bodies were talking to each other all the time—Mrs. B's caresses, Doc's slipping by me and Mrs. B in the kitchen, pulling me into the saddle of his hips for a moment before moving on. I felt like I was keeping a big, juicy secret I was just bursting to tell.

"That feels good." I turned my face toward her palm, my eyes meeting hers. They had a light in them and she was giving me a lazy half-smile.

"It's still so hot!" She stretched again, her tank top pulling up to reveal an expanse of belly over her shorts. "Let's go for a swim."

"Okay." I stood up and brushed sand off my legs. "I'll go get a suit on."

Mrs. B grabbed my hand, her slender fingers squeezing mine. "No need. Private beach and the kiddos are gone, remember? Come on."

She peeled off her tank top, standing there topless while she unsnapped her shorts and wiggled them down her hips. I knew I shouldn't have been shy, considering, but something about this felt different, like there was more conscious intent behind it. I just watched her reveal her body, which had become familiar to me, and yet still filled me with a slow, burning need.

"Want some help?" she purred, using the same tone she used with Doc, as she moved toward me, lifting the edge of my t-shirt. I let her, lifting my arms in acquiescence, my eyes never leaving hers except for the brief moment when the material came off over my head. Her fingers brushed over my shoulders as she dropped the shirt to the sand.

I didn't say anything when she knelt, tugging the elastic of my shorts down over my hips, pulling my panties with them. I just looked down at her, seeing her eyes moving between my legs. The sun turned her hair a fiery gold and made the light in her eyes seem even brighter.

"Hm, need to shave again," she murmured, standing and letting me step out of the shorts at my feet. "Want me to help you later?"

I nodded as she took my hands, pulling me closer so we were standing belly-to-belly, our breasts touching. I wanted her to kiss me, and I think she knew it. She smiled, squeezing my hands and then turned toward the water.

"Last one in is a rotten egg!" She ran toward the shoreline. I only watched her for a moment, her sleek, tawny body streaking toward the water, and then I was after her, both of us tumbling into the surf, laughing and clutching each other in the waves.

Wet, our bodies slid together, and I'm not even sure how it happened, but we were wrapped around each other and her mouth found mine. Everything was so *soft*—her lips, her breasts pressing into mine, her thigh between my legs, the hair my hands got tangled in at the back of her head. It went on and on, the sun finally slipping down below the horizon as we kissed, moaning into each other's mouths.

"Come here." She pulled my hips forward, lifting me in the water, and I wrapped my legs around her body, pressing in tight. I felt the heat of her pussy against mine, more pronounced with the coolness of the water all around us, and I ground my hips against her as we kissed, making her moan.

Her fingers slipped down there between us, finding me, opening, probing, and I gasped and rocked, wanting more. My clit throbbed with that dull ache, like it would never stop. I wiggled and pressed against her, rubbing my breasts into hers, feeling my little nipples sliding wetly over the fullness of her chest.

She lifted me out of the water a little bit, her hands moving over my back, her mouth finding my nipples, sucking first one and then the other. I moaned, my legs wrapped just below her breasts, feeling them pressed hard into my belly.

Writhing and twisting on her as she made fast circles with her tongue around my hard nipples, I threw her off balance, and we tumbled into the water, both of us crying out. I came up sputtering and laughing and she did too, wiping salt water out of her eyes. Still, I reached for her, not wanting it to end, not wanting it to go back to the secret silence of just a few hours before. She took me in, kissing me again, sucking at my tongue, more urgent now.

"Come on." She led me toward shore. "We're safer on the beach."

I giggled, following her as we kicked up sand, which was still warm but cooling now that the sun had set. She spread a large blanket and laid down on it, pulling me with her. Our bodies were still slippery wet and she tasted like salt water when we kissed. Her thigh slipped up over mine as we lay on our sides, my hands moving slowly, tentative now, over her shoulders, her arms, her back.

She looked at me in the dim light, her hand moving down to cup my little breast, moving her thumb over the nipple and making me shiver. Then her tongue followed her fingers, making those same circles over my wet flesh. I felt her breasts pressing into my side and, reaching my fingers down, found a fat brown nipple and squeezed it.

"Oh God, yes!" She arched her back. Encouraged, I rolled it, tugged on it, rubbed my palm over it, and she moaned louder against my breasts, licking them faster, back and forth between them now.

"Oh Mrs. B!" I moaned when her hand slipped down between my legs, her fingers opening me up again, finding my center. My pussy was a hot pulse against her palm.

"I think you can call me Carrie," she murmured as she slipped a finger inside and I flushed at the thought. I couldn't even imagine calling her by her first name—still!—even with her hand rocking over my mound, her fingers, two now, moving in and out me. I found her other nipple, making her groan when I tugged at it, so fat and hard between my thumb and finger.

She kissed her way down my belly and when I realized where she was headed, my whole body filled with anticipation. My skin was still beaded with water and the air felt cool now the sun was gone. Her fingers never stopped moving in the darkness, seeking the heat at my core as her tongue slipped down my smooth, flat belly, and then over the swell of my thighs.

"Oh God," I whispered, rocking against her hand, staring up at the blue velvet sky. "Please." She knew what I was asking for and slipped her fingers out of me, pressing my legs back with her palms. I opened them for her, feeling a little less exposed in the near-dark, hanging onto my knees as I spread wide for her tongue.

"Such a pretty pussy," she breathed, the heat of her words burning through me, and then she licked me, her tongue finding my clit and focusing right there, a wet little flicker that went on and on. I pulled back more, lifting my hips, and she seemed to understand, sliding her fingers back inside of me, twisting them as she started to move in and out.

"Yes," I hissed, her tongue sending the most delicious sensations along my spine. "Oh God, Mrs. B, finger me, do it hard."

She groaned, the vibration of her voice moving right through me as her fingers moved faster, harder, slamming into me as she worked my clit with her tongue. I rolled my head from side to side, dizzy with the feeling, wanting it to last forever and knowing I couldn't possibly hold out against the soft lapping of her tongue, the pounding of her fingers into my pelvis.

"So close," I whispered, and that made her lick faster, fuck me harder, making those little encouraging noises in her throat that sent shivers through me. My pussy was swollen and wet under her mouth. I felt the mix of my juices and her saliva running down my ass toward the blanket.

"Ohhhhhhh now, now!" I cried, unable to keep it back any more.

It came like a tidal wave, sweeping over and drowning me in my own pleasure until I gasped for air, shuddering and arching against her mouth, her fingers still working between my thighs. It moved through me so long I thought I was going to die right there, spread open on a blanket with Mrs. B's face buried between my legs. Then it began to ebb, in hot, pulsing waves, like a tide slowly receding.

"Good girl," she whispered against my pussy, feathering kisses all over my mound, giving me goose bumps. Staring, panting up at the sky, I saw the stars just starting to come out. I pulled at her, wanting her, and she came up and kissed me so I could taste me in her mouth. Sucking on her tongue, I groaned, feeling her breasts pressing into my side.

"Let's go get all this sand and salt water off," she whispered into my ear, nuzzling my neck.

"What about... Doc?" I was still breathless, dazed, floating.

"He'll be gone for hours," she assured me, standing and holding out her hand. "He and Tom Holmes are going out to play pool."

I took her hand, letting her help me stand, and she kissed me again, her mouth greedy, telling me how much more she wanted, and I wanted it, too. We both shivered when we entered the air-conditioning and brushed off as much sand as we could before we ran naked up the stairs to the bathroom. I felt a little more shy in the light, with her eyes on me, even though they were warm and kind...and hungry.

"What are you doing?" I watched as she started the water in the tub instead of the shower.

"I thought a bath would be nice." She sat on the edge and felt the water. I couldn't take my eyes off her body, the full, lush brown curves, the way her hair shone even when it was wet. "Don't you think?"

"Sure." I leaned against the counter and watched as she took a lighter and started illuminating candles all around the tub. When she was finished, she said, "Turn out the light, would you?" I complied, the room going from stark to warm immediately, the candles casting shadow circles on the ceiling.

"What's that?" I watched her pour something from a bottle into the water.

"Bubble bath." She let the tub fill and went out to get us towels. I sat on the edge of the tub, trailing my hand in the warmth and stirring the bubbles around. The scent of lavender filled the room. I didn't say anything when she got a new disposable razor from the drawer and set it on the lip of the tub, but my pussy responded, remembering the last time she'd shaved me down there.

"Come on." She slid past me and stepped over the edge into the half-full tub. I swung my legs over, slipping down into the warm water with a sigh. I'd been dying to soak in this tub since we arrived, but I hadn't ever imagined I'd be doing it with Mrs. B!

"Come here." She gathered me into her. I rested my cheek under her chin, the bubbles making our skin slippery wet. The tub was almost full now with us in it, and I saw the tops of her breasts floating in the water, her nipples hidden under the suds.

"Talented toes!" I laughed when she used her red-painted toes to turn the handles and stop the water.

"You have no idea." She grinned, using her big toe to push the button and turn on the jets, making the bubbles rise even higher. The water rushed around us, soothing, warm, and I sighed happily.

We lay that way for a while, breathing together, watching the shadows flicker over the walls and each other's faces. She played with a wet strand of my hair, wrapping it around her finger. It should have been awkward, but somehow it wasn't. I felt something moving between us, like light or heat, growing with every breath.

"Let's get washed," she murmured into my hair, sitting up in the big tub and reaching for a bottle of shampoo. I closed my eyes and let her scrub and rinse my hair, and then did the same for her, the blonde mass over her shoulders spilling like wet waves of gold. Then she found the soap. It was the moisturizing kind, and she grabbed a scrubby, pouring some on and lathering it up.

"Turn around." She twirled her finger at me. I obeyed, looking at her over my shoulder as she moved my hair aside and started scrubbing my back. The rough yet smooth texture of the cloth felt good, and her hands felt even better as her palms traced everywhere it had been, as if she were smoothing the way.

She turned me toward her, then, moving it down over my shoulders, over my breasts, having me kneel up so she could do my belly. Then she wanted me to stand, and the rough cloth moved over my thighs, between my legs, making me moan a little and spread for her.

"Good." She moved it gently between my lips, her eyes on mine. "Turn around and bend over."

"But—" There was really no real protest left in me. I turned, putting my palms on the edge of the tub, bending over and spreading my legs. I felt her working the cloth over my hips and my ass, her hands following.

"Oh!" I cried when she slipped it between my ass cheeks, scrubbing a little there, moving it over my pussy. "What—?"

"Shhh." Her hand moved there, down the crack, her finger probing at the tender, virgin hole of my ass. I winced, feeling her slip a finger inside to the first knuckle, turning and pushing and then pulling back out.

"My turn," she murmured, putting her hands on my hips and bringing me back down into the water. I sighed in relief, turning to face her as she handed me the scrubby.

I started with her back, so she couldn't see my eyes roaming over her body, how the sudsy, churning water lapped at her full hips as she knelt up and held her hair out of my way, how the curve of her arm, her back, the sweet indentation at her waist, had my breath coming faster, my hands trembling as I washed her back.

I groaned when she turned around, still holding her hair up, and I knelt in the water like I was worshipping her, and I was, running the soapy cloth over her shoulders and breasts. I couldn't help using my hands, finally feeling the weight of them. She sighed and squirmed when I rubbed my palms over her nipples.

"I wish I had breasts like yours." I looked up at her. She just smiled and shook her head, lifting herself up onto the edge of the tub and opening her thighs, the water running off her in bubbly sheets at first, then fading to streams and little rivulets.

"Here." She opened her lips with two fingers. "Don't forget here."

I nodded, swallowing and approaching her pussy with the cloth, swiping at it, tentative. She sighed deeply and opened wider, and I gave up on the cloth, using my hand to rub soap into the pink flesh between her legs.

"Mmmm yes," she whispered when I found the hood of her clit with my fingers.

I'd never seen another girl up close like this and I couldn't help staring, watching how the folds seemed to want to swallow my fingers. She was so smooth, so soft! I wondered if the folds would want to swallow my tongue like that and the thought made me hot all over.

"Don't forget this." She smiled, standing and bending over like I had for her. I gasped, finding the cloth again, washing her bottom and slipping it between the crack of her firm, rounded ass. She spread wider, looking back at me, smiling.

"Go ahead," she said. "Do it."

I bit my lip, but I obeyed, pressing one finger to the tiny, puckered hole of her ass. Her skin was so brown that the hole there looked incredibly pink, and it gave way to my probing as I slid in up to my first knuckle, mimicking her motion, round and round. Mrs. B moaned and pressed back a little, sliding my finger all the way in.

Shocked, I took it back out again, quickly, staring up at her.

"Let's get you shaved." She smiled like she knew a secret she wasn't telling me. Patting the side of the tub, she took the razor and waited for me to open my legs for her.

She used just soap this time, no shaving cream, lathering my pussy up with her whole hand. I moaned, not shy this time about how good it felt. It was over very quickly compared to last time, the razor all-business as it slicked over my skin, leaving smoothness in its wake.

Then she pulled me back into the tub and we knelt together in the swirling water, our mouths slanting, our tongue meshing and my pussy begging to be touched again after her fingers had probed and prodded it during my shave.

"Want to see something?" she whispered against my lips and I nodded. "Watch."

She moved to the side of the tub, grasping onto the edge and opening her knees. I watched as she rocked, eyes closed, moaning a little. At first I was confused, but then I realized what she was doing—the jet from the Jacuzzi was pointing straight between her thighs.

"Try it," Mrs. B murmured, and I saw her nipples, how hard they were, how the water frothed and foamed between her legs. There was a jet right next to her and I grabbed onto the edge, opening my knees like she was, positioning myself over the—

"Oh God!" I cried as the water pulsed against my clit, much harder and faster than any shower massage. Mrs. B was already breathing fast, her hips rolling with the water.

"Isn't it good?" she murmured, and as I watched, she lifted her legs out of the water, dangling them over the edge so she could press her pussy full against the jet. I did it, too, gasping at the intensity of the sensation.

"Oh God, oh God, oh God," I whispered, over and over, the water around us sloshing as we rocked together, the jets gushing in a wicked pulse against our throbbing pussies.

"Oh yeah," Mrs. B moaned, shuddering all over, her voice low and throaty as she threw her head back and I knew she was coming. I wasn't far behind her, my pussy contracting as if it could pull the water right inside of me.

I felt shy again when we got out but she rubbed me dry with a towel without any words and then I rubbed her dry, too. We found our way to her room and stretched out on her bed, lying on our backs, our thighs and arms brushing. It reminded me of that very first day when we were lying out in the sun and remembering took my breath away. Things had come so far, so fast.

I turned toward her, up on my elbow, looking down at her body in the lamplight. Her skin was simply golden and she seemed to glow. I touched her nipple, watching it purse, hearing her sigh and shift, her eyes still closed. I touched the other one, rolling it a little, eliciting a little "mmmm" from her. Growing more bold, I kissed the fat, brown nipple closest to me, gentle at first, and then using my tongue, sucking the bud into my lips.

Mrs. B moaned, her hand tangled in my wet hair as I licked at her nipple, tweaking the other one in my fingers. Her response made my pussy clench and release and I moved my body onto hers, straddling her thighs. Our bodies were soft and fragrantly clean from the bath and her skin tasted new in my mouth as I licked my way down her belly, her hands pressing gently, guiding me.

I was a little afraid, knowing what she wanted, wanting to give it to her and still unsure. In spite of our bath, I could still smell her musky scent as I licked past her navel and moved between her thighs. She spread them wide for me, using her fingers to part her flesh, showing me. I could see much better in the lamplight, how smoothly soft she was, how pink her inside.

Fascinated, I moved her fingers aside and probed with my own, opening her lips, first the outer ones, then the inner ones. The little hole to her pussy gaped slightly when I did, and I bit my lip when I remembered Doc putting his cock inside there. Her pussy was bigger than mine, fuller, the lips fatter and more fleshy. Her inner lips hid way up inside, and her clit was a tiny bud at the top. I touched it and she gasped, rocking a little.

Encouraged by her response, I explored her with my fingers, spreading the wetness seeping out of hole up through her lips and over the hood of her clit. I even pulled the little hood back to see her clit, such a small thing. When I kissed it, she moaned, her hands going to her own breasts, pinching her nipples, and I decided to stay there, kissing, licking, sucking.

She tasted clean and sweet at first but grew more musky and tart as I continued to work her clit with my tongue. I wasn't sure I was doing it right, but she moaned and rocked and her head went back and forth, and I thought it was at least okay. I tried to remember what she'd done to me, out there on the blanket, to send me into orbit, and began flicking my tongue fast, faster, back and forth over the hard little nub of flesh.

"Oh God, yes!" she cried out. "Put your fingers in me!"

I obeyed, searching for the hole, not able to see, finding it and pressing in, first one finger, then two, pumping in and out like she had done to me. She moved against me, rocking, rolling, moving so much it was hard to keep my mouth on her pussy, but I managed, moving with her. My pussy wanted to be touched and I went up on my knees, exposing it, feeling how cool the air was over my heat.

"Come on," she practically growled, her hips bucking. "Fuck me! Fuck me hard, baby!"

I whimpered against her mound, shoving my fingers in deep, slamming them against her, the sound a wet squelching rhythm pounding faster and faster into her flesh. She moaned and squeezed her breasts, pulling at the nipples again and again.

"Make me come!" She grabbed my hair and pulled me into her so hard I could barely breathe. I licked and licked, making my own low moaning sounds against her, my pussy so wet I felt it dripping down my thighs.

"Ah fuck yes, yes, oh God!" She was coming. I felt the fast flutter of her pussy around my fingers, the way her clit seemed to swell and then retreat against my tongue. She was trembling with it, her toes curling on the bed, her hips lifting into my mouth.

When she collapsed, gasping, she moaned again, and I saw her soft, golden belly still quivering with the signs of her pleasure. I rested my cheek against the impossible softness of her thigh, panting myself, trying to calm my own racing heart.

"Oh God, that was so good, sweetie." She stroked my hair, her eyes still closed.

That's when I heard Doc's voice from behind me. "It sure looked good."

We both turned to see him standing in the doorway, staring at us with those dark eyes full of lust. How long had he been watching? I wondered, seeing him walk toward the bed, and then I realized it didn't matter. He wasn't going to be watching anymore.

Chapter Nine

I never told anyone about what happened with the Baumgartners—maybe I just couldn't make it come out in a way that didn't sound sordid. I tried, a few times, but never quite got the right words. I didn't know how to convey all of the feelings underneath, how huge it all seemed, not just enormous, but titanic. I didn't have words big to contain it.

I felt like that when the secret finally came out between us, the moment that Doc crossed the room and sat on the edge of the bed where Mrs. B and I were laying. The jig was up, the game was over, it was all clear from that moment on what we were doing and what we intended to do.

And there weren't words then at first, either. I don't know how that happened, but I remember that we didn't talk. Mrs. B and I snuggled on the bed while we watched him undress. I loved hearing the sound of his belt buckle being undone and would forever get wet when I heard that sound followed by a fast zipper on a pair of tight jeans.

I fit my head under Mrs. B's chin and traced figure 8's around her navel while Doc pulled off his t-shirt and tossed it in the pile with his jeans and his boxer briefs, and then he was with us, between us, a warm, solid presence that our eyes met and smiled over as we cuddled on the bed.

I felt shy now, a little awkward, not knowing how to proceed, what to say, and so I didn't say anything. I just let it all flow, and that's exactly what happened. Mrs. B was humming something—she did that a lot, little snippets of songs—and Doc was stroking her hair, and then he was stroking mine, too, petting us both, making us purr.

I started humming along, following the motion of Mrs. B's fingers as she traced circles on Doc's belly. Our circles grew closer until our fingers touched, and then our hands touched, and then our mouths touched as we leaned in to kiss each other over him. I felt his hand in my hair, and I saw his hand in hers, and then he was touching my shoulder, my arm, his fingers light and tender over my skin.

Mrs. B moaned against my mouth and I saw Doc's hand cupping her breast, thumbing her nipple, making it hard. Watching him do that while she began to breathe harder against the soft curve of my neck, her lips sucking and nibbling there, made me feel faint. His hand rubbed slowly up and down my arm and I turned my head and put it against Mrs. B's shoulder, feathering kisses there as my eyes met Doc's. He was watching, his eyes moving over both of us like he couldn't take in enough.

I glanced down at where he was cupping Mrs. B's breast, the flesh overflowing his fingers, and I reached for his other hand, the one caressing my shoulder, and placed it over my little breast. He smiled, his palm moving over my flesh, lifting it and letting it fall. I moaned when he starting thumbing my nipple, too, the sensation riding every nerve pathway that ended at my throbbing clit.

With a sigh and whimper, I nuzzled Mrs. B's neck, and we were licking and sucking and gently biting each other, my dark hair tangling with her blonde mane, a cloud of still-damp softness. That's when I saw that Mrs. B had her hand wrapped around Doc's hard cock. She was squeezing and tugging it, real easy and slow.

Fascinated, I watched, seeing how red the tip was already, how it throbbed in her hand.

Her mouth found mine again and we kissed, pressing in a little closer over Doc's chest, our breasts touching. I moaned when I felt him rubbing our nipples together, my little pink point and her thick, brown bud kissing just like we were, lost in sensation. I squirmed and sucked at Mrs. B's tongue and she teased me, pulling it back and then letting me have it again.

Then Mrs. B broke the kiss and gave me that little half-smile, leaning over and kissing the dark line of hair that ran from Doc's navel down to his crotch. I watched, biting my lip as she kissed the tip of his cock. His hand was still cupping my breast, teasing my nipple. I glanced at him, then at her, wanting and not knowing how to say it or what to do.

Mrs. B's mouth slid around the head, making Doc groan and shift a little, his thigh moving against mine. She smiled at me, a thin strand of saliva running from her lower lip to the tip of his cock, and crooked her finger in a "come here" gesture. I slid down the bed next to her and Doc made room between his legs for the both of us, his eyes moving between our faces.

She didn't say anything, but she offered his cock to me, and I couldn't help remembering the first day I saw it—Doc stroking it out on the balcony while he watched us lying topless on the beach together. I never thought then that I would be doing this now, but here I was, leaning in to kiss the head, running my tongue around the ridge, my pussy clenching when Doc moaned and looked at me like I was a dream.

Mrs. B put her head next to mine, our eyes meeting over her husband's engorged cock, and then she kissed me around it, our lips on the swollen head, our tongues searching for each other. Doc moaned again and I felt his hand in my hair as Mrs. B slowly stroked his shaft while our mouths worked over the glans. We both tugged on it, sucking it, fighting over it, like two kittens with a new toy.

I found myself greedy, aching to feel him fully in my mouth and nudged her out of the way, taking his cock down my throat. He gasped and I looked up at him as I swallowed more, and more still, hearing Mrs. B chuckle, her tongue moving at the base of him and then lower, down to his balls. Fascinated, I watched her lick and suck them as Doc pressed me lower onto his cock. He was thick and throbbing and I loved the velvety feel of his skin against my tongue.

Mrs. B cupped his balls, rolling them in her hands, her eyes on me as she sucked one of his testicles into her mouth. I watched, wide-eyed, as I came up on Doc's shaft, licking just around the head, teasing it with my tongue.

"Wanna try?" Mrs. B asked, her voice low, a little throaty, holding his sac up, offering it to me. Nodding, I slid down fully, my tongue running over the soft, ridged skin while she grabbed and squeezed his cock. Doc shaved down there and the skin was completely smooth. I heard him whisper something, but I couldn't make out the words, although I could tell they were full of pleasure and that thrilled me.

His balls were getting tighter, drawing up closer to his body as Mrs. B continued to stroke him, making them harder to suck into my mouth and roll around with my tongue. I nibbled a little on the skin and Doc jumped, his eyes wide as he looked down at me.

"Sorry." I bit my lip.

He smiled and crooked his finger at me like she had. "Come here."

I crawled up onto him and he pulled me in against his chest, grabbing my ass with his hand. "Maybe you deserve a spanking?"

"Doc!" I laughed when his hand slapped my ass. It stung a little, but then he kissed me and I was lost in it, his tongue seeking mine, his cock hard against my thigh, Mrs. B's hand still moving it up and down.

"Did you like my cock in your mouth?" he whispered in my ear, kissing my cheek, my neck, sending shivers through me.

"Yes," I whispered back, feeling his fingers tugging at my nipple again, making me squirm.

"Do you want to feel it in your little pussy?" He slid his hand down over my belly, his palm cupping my soft, shaved mound.

Moaning, I rocked against him. "Yes."

He chuckled, parting my flesh there, slipping one of his big fingers between my lips. I was soaking wet and he slid easily through, finding my clit and petting it.

"Tell me." He met my eyes. I hesitated, looking down at Mrs. B, who stroked him as she watched us, her breasts swaying prettily to the rhythm. Then I looked back at him, feeling shy and shaking my head as I bit my lip.

He smiled again, teasing me. "Go on... say it... 'I want you to fuck me.'"

"Doc!" I felt his finger slip in me, exploring the soft, smooth walls inside. "Please."

"Do you like that?" He pushed his fingers deeper. I moaned, nodding, hiding my blush against his neck. He pressed another one in, stretching me wider, making me gasp and wriggle on top of him. "Not as good as a nice big cock, though, is it?"

"No." My hands clutched his shoulders as he began to finger me in earnest, using the force of his arm to shove them up inside of me. I slid my thighs open wider, making room, wanting more. "Oh, God... Doc, please!'

"Come on." He slid out from under me. I sat up, watching as he leaned over and kissed Mrs. B, their tongues meeting, her hand going behind his head to pull him in deeper. She still had his cock in her hand.

He looked over at me, his eyes moving up and down my body, hungry. "Did you like licking Carrie's pussy?"

I still couldn't get used to her as 'Carrie,' but I nodded, my eyes meeting Mrs. B's as I remembered the taste of her, the soft pink flesh melting in my mouth, the way she moaned and shook and thrust.

"You want some more?" He smiled, reaching down and spreading Mrs. B open wide. She groaned, spreading her thighs, letting him slide the fingers that had just been inside of me up into her pussy.

"Yes." I felt a familiar ache between my legs as I watched him fuck her with his fingers.

"Lie down, baby." Doc whispered into her hair, kissing the top of her head. She did as she was told, lying on her back sideways on the bed next to me, giving me a smile. She was close enough to touch me, and she did, reaching out and cupping my cheek with her palm, her slender fingers moving over my jaw and then down my shoulder.

"Isn't she beautiful, Doc?" Mrs. B's fingertips brushed my nipple, sending a wave of heat through me.

"Beyond." He squeezed his cock in his own hand now as he watched us.

Mrs. B's fingers roamed further down and I opened my legs for her as she slipped her fingers through my wetness. "Look, she's all smooth for you."

"I see that." He watched her slip a finger inside of me. I sighed and spread a little more for her. "I bet she tastes like the sweetest little peach..."

Mrs. B rubbed her own pussy, too, I saw her fingers moving through her flesh, her breasts moving a little with the motion.

"She does," Mrs. B confirmed with a smile, meeting my eyes. "Come here, Veronica. Let me lick you again."

I hesitated, crawling toward her and groaning when her fingers slipped out of me, not sure where she wanted me, how—and then she grabbed my hips, positioning me over her face, squeezing my ass and pulling my pussy down to her mouth.

"Oh God!" I felt her tongue probing between my lips as I found myself face to face with her mound, her fingers still moving there. "Oh, Mrs. B!"

"I bet she'd like your tongue, too," Doc suggested to me and I looked over at him sitting on the edge of the bed, watching us, slowly pumping his cock through his fist.

Mrs. B moaned when I slipped my tongue between her lips, tasting the sweet juices I'd brought to the surface during her last orgasm. It was so hard to concentrate on what I was doing while her fingers and mouth worked between my legs, driving me to distraction. I just found her clit and focused there, licking in a slow, steady rhythm, my eyes on Doc.

I couldn't help watching him as he looked at us together, listening to our moans, our cries, our whimpers. He started slow, moving the skin up over the head of his cock as he stroked it, and then he pumped harder, so fast that his shaft was a blur and just the wet tip was visible. Then he slowed again, and sometimes he squeezed the head hard, groaning, his eyes closing for a moment.

"Oh, Mrs. B!" I felt her fingers move into me. I remembered how she had liked that and slid my fingers into her, too. She rewarded me with a moan, rocking as I started to fuck her. Her pussy made the sweetest wet sound when I did that, meeting my fingers, sucking them in deeper.

Doc's eyes were on me, watching my tongue and hand, as he slid across the bed toward me. "Open your mouth, Ronnie." He pressed his cock toward my lips.

I did, sucking the wet head into my mouth, groaning around his shaft as he pushed in even further. I kept my fingers in Mrs. B's pussy, making those wet sounds. She focused right on my clit, her tongue lapping faster and faster, and I felt that dizzy feeling I got just before I couldn't stop.

"Move your fingers." Doc groaned when he took his cock out of my mouth. "And spread her open for me."

I gasped, using my fingers to part Mrs. B's fat, swollen lips, showing him the way. He slid his cock into the little gaping hole there, and she moaned against my pussy, her fingers driving deep into me. Doc grabbed her knees, pushing them back toward me as he thrust into her with a grunt, his eyes closing, face taut.

"God!" He opened his eyes and looked down at me. I was trying to lick her, still, my tongue moving over his shaft, too, where it slid between her lips. He pulled out of her, slow, and found my mouth again. I sucked greedily, licking the taste of Mrs. B off of his shaft.

"Whoa, whoa!" He grabbed my hair and pulled me back as I sucked on him. "Easy."

I moaned, Mrs. B's tongue just seconds from taking me over the edge, my mouth full of her juices and the taste of his pre-cum.

"Please, Doc," I panted, my eyes half-closing with my impending orgasm. "I want you to fuck me."

He groaned then, and I felt him shifting, moving on the bed, but I couldn't pay attention because I was coming, Mrs. B's tongue making the most delicious circles over my clit as I shuddered and moaned and spread for her. She cooed and kissed me, still hungry, and I moaned when I felt Doc's hands grabbing my hips.

Looking back over my shoulder, I saw him positioned behind me, felt the fat head of his cock rubbing up and down my slick cleft. I shivered when he brushed my still-sensitive clit before sliding back up and finding my hole. He felt big as he eased in, groaning the whole way, and my pussy still fluttering a little from my climax, squeezing his cock.

"God damn!" He gripped my hips and pressed all the way in. "So tight."

Mrs. B wiggled out from underneath me as I went to my hands and knees. She twisted, turned, moving so that she was under me again. This time we were face-to-face, her eyes on mine. Slipping a hand behind my head, she pulled my mouth to hers and kissed me as I felt Doc begin, pulling his cock almost all the way out before sliding back into me again.

I moaned into her mouth when he really started to fuck me hard, driving me forward against her, my little breasts quivering against hers. He spread my legs wider with his big thighs, pressing me open, thrusting his cock deep, now.

"Do you like that?" Mrs. B whispered into my ear, licking my neck.

I was breathless with it, panting, being fucked so hard. "Yes!" I arched my back. "Oh God, that feels so good."

Mrs. B's hands cupped my breasts, playing with my nipples, and I saw her looking past me and knew she was looking at Doc—I could feel the communication passing between them like heat.

"Tell him," Mrs. B whispered, looking into my half-closed eyes. "Tell him how much you love him fucking you."

I groaned, feeling a heat creeping through my chest. I was lying naked on top of Mrs. B, and Doc was pounding my pussy from behind—how could I possibly be shy? And still, the words felt like too much in my mouth, and I shook my head.

"Please," Mrs. B murmured, reaching down and finding my clit. I groaned as she rubbed it in little baby circles, moving the fleshy hood against the tiny bud underneath.

"Oh God!" I moaned, lifting my hips for him, feeling his cock swelling inside of me, his balls slapping against my pussy with every thrust. "Oh yes, yes," I gasped. "I love your big cock inside of me. Fuck me, Doc! Fuck me, hard!"

He groaned, his fingers digging into my hips. "Damn, she catches on quick!"

Mrs. B kissed me again, her tongue making circles against mine as her fingers made the same delicious shape against my clit. I couldn't believe I was nearing that edge again, but I was. Between the pump and swell of his cock in me and the slick rub of her fingers, I couldn't hold out against them both.

"Oh, I'm gonna come!" I buried my face in her neck. She kissed my hair again and again, her fingers never stopping, and Doc gave me the fullest, hardest thrusts I'd ever had, making me shake all over. I gasped and hissed as my orgasm hit, biting at her shoulder, my pussy clenching tight around the shaft of his cock, pulling him into me.

"Oh fuck!" he cried, and I could actually feel his cock getting bigger inside of me, full to bursting. Mrs. B's hand moved between my legs, pulling on his shaft. He wasn't in me anymore, but he thrust behind me, driving me forward onto her as he came, growling and grunting as he gripped my ass.

Mrs. B smiled at me, lifting her hand to her mouth, and I saw that it was full of Doc's cum. She licked at the side where the white stuff was sliding down her palm and then offered it to me. Hesitant, but remembering the taste of him after he came all over my belly, I licked at her fingers. It was acidic, different from the taste of her, but the look in her eyes and the moan she gave me when I sucked it from between her fingers sent a thrill through me.

"It's all over my pussy," she whispered, a light in her eyes again.

Doc moved from behind me, coming to lie next to Mrs. B with a groan. I smiled, moving down between her legs, and she watched as I started licking the slick, white fluid pooled on her mound. Doc watched, too, incredulous, as I followed a thick strand of it between her lips, sucking her clit into my mouth.

"Oh God!" Her hands went to my hair. I stayed there, my tongue moving back and forth against her clit, the taste of both of them in my mouth as I looked between their faces. Doc cupped her breasts, rolling her nipples, and I felt her whole body tensing, ready.

"Yes!" She trembled with the force of it, hands clenching the comforter into her fists. I couldn't stop licking her—I was so greedy, so hungry—but she made me, pulling me up to her. They both kissed me and then they kissed each other as I snuggled down between them. I had never felt so wanted.

Chapter Ten

Doc's finger traced the outline of my lips. Behind me, Mrs. B's breathing had become deep and even, her chest rising and falling against my back, her arm thrown over my hip. I touched my forehead to his, trying to take it in, and found that I couldn't. It was just too much to digest all at once, and I couldn't do anything but be there, pressed between them, feeling a little like I was flying.

A low, growly sound caught our attention and I flushed. "My stomach."

"Hungry?" He moved his hand to cover my navel.

I nodded. "Starving. We didn't have dinner."

"Well we can't have that." He smiled. "And I'm about to die of dehydration myself. Let's go scrounge."

He rolled out of bed, holding his hand out to me. I slipped out from under Mrs. B's arm, taking his hand and letting him help me stand.

"What about Mrs. B?" I looked back at her. She was sleeping, her hair falling over her face.

Doc put one knee on the bed, leaning over and brushing the hair out of her eyes, kissing her cheek and talking right into her ear. "Baby... Ronnie and I are hungry. Wanna come to the kitchen and get something with us?"

She murmured something unintelligible, rolling over to her other side, reaching back and pulling the comforter with her. He smiled and tucked it around her, kissing her hair.

"Guess not." He grabbed his boxer briefs from a pile of clothes and tugged them on. He noticed me standing there with my arms crossed over my chest. I was a little cold, and a lot shy now, all of a sudden.

"Here you go." He smiled and picked his t-shirt up off the floor, tossing it to me. I followed him out the door, pulling the dark material over my head. It hung to mid-thigh on me, and it smelled like him.

Mrs. B always left the light over the stove on so we could see our way to the kitchen. Doc opened the fridge, grabbing the milk carton and drinking straight from it. I made a face and snorted when his eyes skipped to mine. He lowered the carton, grinning as he wiped his chin with the back of his hand.

"Sorry," he apologized, putting it back and grabbing a glass out of the cupboard.

I just rolled my eyes and said, "Ew," opening the fridge back up. My stomach was really making noise now. Doc was standing at the sink with the water running, just drinking glass after glass. He was swallowing continuously but the angle of the glass made it come so fast his mouth couldn't contain it all and it dribbled out the sides.

"Thirsty?" I teased him, finding a ripe peach in the fruit basket next to the fridge and taking a bite while I rummaged. It was juicier than I expected and I tried to catch it before it ran down my chin onto Doc's shirt.

"Hungry?" Doc teased back, putting his glass back down on the counter and burping loudly.

"Ew!" I said again through a mouthful of peach flesh, rolling my eyes. "Gross!"

He chuckled as the peach juice filled my cupped hand and he tore off a paper towel, handing it to me. I reached for it, but he pulled his hand back with a grin.

"Hey!" I swallowed my next bite of peach. I couldn't stop eating it. My stomach was protesting too loudly. "Gimme that."

"Come get it." He held it above his head.

"Doc!" I reached for it, but he was much too tall for me. I jumped once, trying to grab it and he laughed, keeping it just high enough that I couldn't quite get it.

"You're enjoying this!" I made a face at him.

He laughed again. "Hell yeah, I am."

Grabbing me around the waist, he pulled me close, his mouth covering mine. It felt strange, standing in the kitchen and kissing this way with Mrs. B sleeping upstairs. He licked at my lips, my chin, my neck where all the peach juice had spread.

"Doc…"

His mouth reached the hollow of my throat, lapping at the sweetness there.

"Hmm?" His tongue was dipping below the neckline of the t-shirt, his hands lifting it in back.

"I'm still hungry," I protested with a laugh, pushing at him with one hand, my other still holding the dripping peach.

He groaned, looking at me and licking his lips. "Me, too. And you're sweet."

I rolled my eyes. "Oh, please!"

Smiling, he reached around me and opened the fridge while I devoured the rest of the peach. He started pulling things out.

"Gotta have some protein." He put lunchmeat and cheese onto the counter. "Keep your energy up."

"Ha." I snorted, tossing the peach pit in the garbage under the sink and washing my hands. "Very funny."

"Ok, then, gotta keep *my* energy up." He looked back at me with a grin as I wiped my face and neck with a wet paper towel. "I've got two beautiful women in my bed now."

I flushed and was glad that the stove light wasn't too bright. "I'm still hungry."

"Well, eat!" He waved his hand at the spread on the counter.

I grabbed a slice of ham and a slice of cheese, rolling them together. Doc was making some sort of sandwich, stacking piles of lunchmeat and cheese on bread as I watched.

"Who are you—Dagwood?" I laughed, finishing my first ham and cheese roll-up and making another.

"You're too young to remember Dagwood." He was squirting mustard on the mess.

I smiled. "Yeah, it's an ancient history reference."

He groaned. "Thanks. I'll have you know, *I'm* too young to remember Dagwood."

"Age is a matter of mind," I quipped, finishing my second ham and cheese roll. "I don't mind, so it doesn't matter."

He looked over at me, smiling but there was something else there, and then asked casually, "Are you ok?"

The question stopped me. I didn't know how to answer—I didn't know the answer.

"I think so." I filled a glass with milk and took a long drink. He bit into his sandwich, still standing at the counter, just watching me.

"If you're not, will you tell me?" He swallowed. I noticed some mustard at the corner of his mouth. Somehow his question made me feel warm and soft in the middle.

"Yeah." I nodded, reaching out and touching the dab of mustard with my finger. "You've got something—"

He caught my hand, kissing the inside of my wrist. I smiled, and he kissed up a little higher, and higher still, his eyes on mine.

"Who are you, now—Gomez?" I laughed as he set his sandwich down and kissed fast up to my elbow.

"Tish!" He grinned and wiggled his eyebrows. "You spoke French!"

I giggled as he kissed higher up my arm, over my shoulder.

"No, I didn't!" I felt his lips on my neck. His hands slipped behind me, moving under my shirt.

"I still can't resist you." He kissed me, tasting like mustard and bologna on rye and I put my arms around his neck, stretching up on tiptoe to press myself against him. His fingers gripped my ass, pulling me up to him as our mouths slanted together, his tongue moving with mine.

"Now, I'm hungry." His voice was low as he kissed his way back down my neck, lifting my t-shirt, and I let him pull it off over my head.

"God you're something." He looked at me for a moment, shaking his head a little and smiling. The he grabbed my bottom and lifted me, squealing, to the opposite counter, setting me up on it.

"What are you doing?" I smiled, my eyes dipping down past the top elastic band of his boxer-briefs and seeing the bulge there. It made something in my belly tighten.

"I told you." He sank to his knees on the tile in front of me. "I'm hungry."

"Doc..." My hand moved through his hair as his palms spread my thighs. "We can't—"

He pulled me forward, hooking my legs over his shoulders, breathing me in.

"Spread it for me." His breath was hot against my mound. Biting my lip, I did as I was told, reaching down and opening my lips with two fingers. He made an "mmm" sound and looked up at me.

"Show me," he said. "Play with your pussy."

I slipped my finger over to my clit, rubbing it a little, pressing the hood up and down, back and forth. It was only a few moments before everything there began to tingle and I was making a soft "mmm" sound, too.

"Do you finger yourself?" His eyes following the path of my fingers through my lips and back up to my clit.

"Sometimes." I put my feet up on his shoulders, giving him a better view and spreading myself really wide. He groaned as he watched me slide a finger into my pussy, and then another, moving them slowly in and out and using my thumb against my clit.

"Talented girl," he murmured, and I saw his shoulder and arm muscles moving and knew that he was rubbing his cock. When I slid my fingers out and back up to my clit, he grabbed my wrist, sucking the juices off.

"My turn." He licked my swollen lips, up one side, then the other, teasing me at the top of the cleft, pulling on the skin with his tongue but not touching my clit.

I slid my hands over my breasts, my nipples so hard they felt hot under my fingers as I rolled and tugged on them, sending sweet waves of extra pleasure down to the spot that Doc was licking with his tongue. He moved it around and around at first—fat, lazy circles that made me moan and press my feet into his shoulders.

Then his fingers moved inside of me, twisting, searching, exploring the smooth, tight walls of my pussy. His mouth covered my clit, his tongue doing that fast flutter back and forth that I heard learned to love so much, and I wondered if Mrs. B liked it, too, or if she had told him about it. Then I couldn't think at all anymore as turned his fingers in me, palm up, and crooked them, like he had earlier when he told me to "come here."

At first, there was just the pressure of his fingers, stroking there inside of me as his mouth covered my mound, his tongue working between my legs. Then it felt like I had to pee and I tried to make him stop, wiggling and squirming, but he wouldn't let me go, he just kept on and on, harder, even, rubbing that spot deep inside me as he licked my clit.

"Doc!" I felt something coming and I was almost scared by the intensity of it. He made a noise in his throat, his eyes on mine, nodding against me as his tongue moved faster still, his fingers inside me digging deeper, rubbing, rubbing, until I thought I would die.

"Oh fuck!" I nearly screamed it as something let go, completely let go, and I was coming buckets, flooding him with my juices as my pussy spasmed around his fingers, trying to draw him in deeper. My clit was just a hot, throbbing button of pleasure sending waves through me until my limbs felt weak and trembling with it.

"Oh my God," I whispered, looking down at him, my climax still pulsing through my body. "Oh my God, oh my God, oh my God."

I gasped when he stood, and I saw the front of him was soaked, just covered with me. I looked at him in horror, covering my mouth.

"It's okay." He pulled me close and I wrapped myself around him. "That's supposed to happen."

"It is?" I looked up at him, doubtful. He nodded, kissing me, and I could taste my pussy and something else, something sweet.

"I told you I was hungry." He grabbed my ass and pulled me in toward the bulge in his crotch. His boxers were still on and I reached down between us, feeling the lump of hard heat there.

"Now it's my turn?" I smiled, rubbing my hand over it.

He groaned. "Be my guest."

I slid off the counter, letting him lean against it as I freed his cock, yanking his shorts down and tossing them aside. He stood straight out, pulsing slightly in my hand, and I slid the head past my lips, running my tongue all around it like I'd seen Mrs. B do. His cock was big and hard to get down my throat, but I tried, swallowing more of it every time I went down on him again.

By the time I was taking a little more than half of him into my mouth, he was breathing harder, his hands were in my hair, and he moaned a little, his eyes closed, his head back. Remembering Mrs. B sucking his balls earlier that night, I reached under and cupped them, rolling them gently in my hands.

"Oh God yeah!" He groaned and I saw his eyes roll back a little as he took a long, deep breath. "You are such a sweet little cock sucker."

The praise and the dirty words went through me like white heat, making my pussy buzz. I sucked harder then, wanting to please him, hear him moan louder, and was rewarded when he grabbed my hair, pulling me off his cock. It made a fat "pop" as it came out, my saliva still dripping from the end.

"I want to fuck you!" he growled and I nodded, standing, my hand reaching for his cock again, wanting it.

"Where?" I looked around.

"Right fucking here!" He turned me and pressed my belly into the counter.

I didn't have time to think as he parted my lips with the fat head of his cock from behind, forcing his way through my wet flesh. I gripped the edge of the counter to keep my balance as he started to fuck me, his cock slamming into me, his fingers digging into my hips.

"God, I love your tight little cunt!" He groaned, fucking me a little deeper, using his legs to come up into me at an angle, making me squeal. The sound of his words were like music, and it made my body sing.

"Fuck me, Doc!" I pressed my cheek to the counter, letting him take me.

"Say it again." He grunted, moving his hips in small circles now, staying deep, rubbing the swollen head of his cock somewhere in my depths.

"Oh God!" I cried, going up on my tiptoes, spreading as wide as I could to take him and still wanting more. "Fuck me, Doc! Fuck me, hard!'

"Good girl!" he growled, and he did fuck me harder, and I didn't even know he could, his cock pistoning into my pussy, his pelvis slapping fast against my ass, making my breath hitch.

"Oh God, oh God, oh God!" I cried, over and over, feeling him filling me, stretching me open, his cock spearing into my slick, aching tunnel and still I held on, squeezing him, wanting more, wanting it to go on and on.

"Come on, baby." He reached under and found my clit, making me whimper. "Do it for me, Ronnie."

"Oh Doc!" I moaned, not able to stand against it, his fingers working me, his cock impaling me, I was lost, and I came hard, shuddering with the force of it, feeling my belly quiver and tremble against the smooth, cool counter underneath me. He rode it with me, my pussy squeezing him, threatening to swallow his shaft, until I gasped and panted under him.

"Now..." He eased me up and back, still inside of me. "I want you to swallow it all like a good hungry little girl."

I turned and sank to my knees, sucking and licking all my juices off his cock. It wasn't long, a few hard thrusts deep into my throat, and he shuddered and filled my mouth with his cum. There was so much of it I thought I would choke, and I couldn't do anything but swallow and swallow, my eyes and throat burning with the intensity of it.

He slid out of my mouth, still wet, and sank to his knees, too, rocking me, murmuring something I couldn't quite hear because my ears were still ringing.

"Still hungry?" he asked after a moment.

I laughed and looked up at him, sliding my hand between his legs and squeezing his softening cock.

"Yes."

Chapter Eleven

I woke up stretched out naked on my tummy in the Baumgartner's bed, the early morning light streaming in the window. I smelled coffee and heard the shower running and saw a pillow on either side of me where they had slept. I stretched, flushing when I remembered last night—not just our midnight snack, but later, coming to bed with Mrs. B, the way they pressed me between them when they kissed.

I couldn't count how many times I had woken up to feel his hand or hers between my legs or cupping my breast. Once it was his cock pressed between my cheeks from behind while Mrs. B held my leg up so he could fuck me, slow and easy. I felt dazed and sleepy, but I remembered coming while Mrs. B rubbed my clit and sucked my nipples.

I sat up and glanced in the vanity mirror, my hair a dark bed-head cloud. I smoothed it, rubbing my eyes, and stood, grabbing onto the edge of the bed. My thighs were sore, and between my legs was a little sore, too. *How many times did we—?* I touched myself down there, feeling the slickness of my juices and Doc's cum. *How many times did he—?* I lifted it to my fingers, smelling it, and then licked it. It was a taste I was growing to like.

Heading toward my room, I saw the bathroom door open and heard their voices. The shower was still running, and Mrs. B was talking.

"We can't stay any longer, Doc. Christmas is just around the corner, and I know she's got school starting up again."

I edged toward the door, seeing the steam buildup near the ceiling.

Doc sighed. "Maybe we can come out for winter break in February?"

"Maybe." I could see Mrs. B's curvy form behind the clear shower curtain, her hands moving over her breasts and down her belly. "I guess we'll see."

"My winter break starts February twenty-first," I volunteered from the doorway, surprised at my own candor.

Doc poked his dark, wet head around the curtain, giving me a smile. "Hey there, sleepyhead. Wanna join us?"

"I definitely need a shower." I stepped toward him, noticing the way his eyes moved over my body as he held the curtain open for me.

"There's our girl." Mrs. B held out her hand to me. I stepped between them, the hot water making me wince a little as I got used to the temperature. "Sleep well?"

I flushed, remembering how many times we'd been up together during the night. "When I was sleeping... yeah."

She smiled and I felt Doc move in closer behind me, pressing me into Mrs. B's curves. Putting her arms around my waist, she pulled me in, rubbing her soft belly against mine. I closed my eyes at the sensation, tilting my head back a little and getting my hair wet under the showerhead.

"Want me to wash it?" Mrs. B volunteered, already pushing the shampoo button. They had those automatic dispensers in the shower.

I turned for her, facing Doc and feeling her fingers massaging my scalp. He just watched, a small smile playing on his lips, but when she tilted my head forward to do the back, I saw his cock was pointing straight at me. Even after the more than satisfying night before, the sight of it still thrilled me. I reached out and slid my hand around the head, moving my thumb over the mushroom-like tip.

"Maybe I should wash the rest of you?" Doc offered, his voice low as he pumped some soap into his hands. They had an automatic dispenser for that, too.

Mrs. B grabbed the shower massage and had me tilt my head back so she could rinse my hair. Doc's hands moved over my neck and shoulders, his big palms rubbing and massaging. I moaned out loud, feeling an instant sense of my body relaxing under his touch. I hadn't known any of my muscles were tight.

He massaged all the way down my arms to my fingertips and then turned me to face Mrs. B, working his thumbs and palms down my back. Mrs. B stepped in close and I leaned my head on her shoulder as Doc made his way over my hips and ass. His hands were large and firm, and I didn't know how clean I was getting, but it felt fantastic.

Mrs. B was pressing into me, too, her breasts slippery against mine, her smooth thigh sliding between my legs. I let her support me, wrapping my arms around her as Doc's hands made their way down my sore legs. The muscles there actually quivered under his fingers as he worked his way from my knees up my inner thighs.

"Turn around," Doc said, and I did, leaning back against Mrs. B who was kissing and sucking on my neck, giving me goose bumps even in the warmth of the shower.

I watched his eyes moving down my body with his hands, soaping up my breasts, massaging them, too, tweaking my nipples and making them hard. His fingers worked over my ribcage, my waist, pressing in at my hips and pelvis, and then reached between my legs.

"Easy," I murmured, wincing. "I'm a little sore." I felt Mrs. B's chuckle more than heard it as she slid her hands around me now, cupping my breasts.

"Poor Ronnie." Doc slid his soapy fingers between my tender lips. In spite of the slight soreness, his fingers felt good, rubbing back and forth over my swollen pussy and I couldn't help responding with a little moan. He grabbed the shower massage Mrs. B put back, turning it onto my pussy and making it pulse.

"Oh!" My head went back onto Mrs. B's shoulder. She made a little "mmm" sound as she rolled my nipples in her fingers. Doc focused it right on my clit, the water pumping hard as he pressed it in. He moved closer, pinning me between them, his mouth finding mine, the water still rushing between my legs, making me quiver.

His cock was hard against my thigh and I grabbed it, pulling on it, and he groaned into my mouth, his tongue finding mine as he turned the shower massage even higher. That was too much, and in just a few seconds, I was gasping with my orgasm, sucking his tongue into my mouth and pumping his cock as I came, feeling Mrs. B's full, slick, slippery body behind me as I rocked.

He turned the shower massage off, and then the water. Mrs. B held me, kissed me, her mouth soft and warm as I turned to kiss her back, my hands moving up her ribcage to her breasts. I loved the weight of them, how they burst out of my fingertips no matter how I held them.

Doc pulled the shower curtain open, grabbing a towel and drying himself off as he watched us. Mrs. B was lifting her breast for me to kiss and lick and suck and I did, making her moan and loving the sound.

"God you two are so beautiful together," he murmured, and I glanced over at him, seeing his hand moving over his stiff cock out of the corner of my eye. Mrs. B lifted the other breast and pressed them together, pointing the nipples towards each other. I could lick them both at once that way, and I did, hearing her groan and watching her eyes close, her head go back.

I loved the sound of her pleasure and it made me want to taste her, to lick her until toes and fists curled and she shuddered under my mouth. She pulled me up to her and we kissed again, her tongue exploring, searching.

Doc pulled us out of the shower, giving us towels, and we dried each other, still stopping to kiss. Then we were belly to belly again, her leg wrapped around me, her foot hooked behind my knee, the soft cries and whimpers we made echoing the softness of our bodies rubbing together.

"Look." Doc came to stand next to us, nudging us toward the sinks. There was a long mirror there, and we were all reflected in it, Doc behind me and Mrs. B. "Look how beautiful you two are together."

We looked at each other in the mirror, Mrs. B and I, our eyes meeting and smiling. Doc's hands moved down our backs, over our asses, squeezing, looking in the mirror at us and shaking his head. I think it thrilled him more than it did us, because we turned together again, kissing and touching each other while he watched.

Mrs. B spread a towel up on the counter and slid onto it, pulling me between her legs. I kissed her again and she breathed me in, her tongue flicking over the tip of mine, and I knew the motion already, knew exactly what she was suggesting and wanted. I kissed my way down over her shoulders, licking away some of the water still beaded there, and then cupped her breasts in my hands.

I couldn't resist them on the way down and she moaned when I pressed them together, just like she had, making the nipples touch so I could lick them both. Doc watched, leaning back against the counter, his cock hard in his fist and I smiled over at him in mid-lick and then sucked both of her nipples into my mouth.

"Oh!" she cried, going back onto her elbows.

I followed, my pussy rubbing against hers as I stretched out and leaned over her, my tongue working back and forth over the thick, firm flesh of her nipples. I couldn't help rocking against her, my pussy filled with that ache again, but it was all the wrong angle, just a tease, our smooth lips rubbing, the swell of our thighs in the way.

"Try this," Doc murmured, seeing my frustration, lifting my leg and putting it onto the counter over Mrs. B's thigh. That was a little better, and I could wiggle and mash my lips more fully with hers, but I couldn't reach her breasts from this angle. She took over where I left off, rolling her nipples as I made circles over her pussy with mine. It still wasn't quite good enough—my clit was aching for more.

The bathroom counter was big, but I wasn't sure if it was wide enough for both of us. That's what I wanted—to be up on top of her. Doc moved in behind me, helping me, lifting my leg, hers, pushing us onto the counter, so Mrs. B leaned back against the mirror. Then I knelt over her, one thigh between hers, the other hooked over her hip, the soft flesh of our pussies sliding over each other.

"Oh yes!" Mrs. B's gaze moved first to Doc, who held me, making sure I wouldn't fall, then to me, her eyes starting to close with the sensation.

She reached down and spread her lips open, mine too, her fingers pushing and prodding at our flesh until our clits kissed as I rocked on her. I felt faint the moment my little bud touched hers, gasping out loud and feeling myself go weak. Doc held me, urging me, rocking me, and I kept going, seeing our reflection in the mirror.

His hand went to my nipples, and mine went to hers, tweaking, rolling, pulling, sending sweet waves down to where we were rubbing together. I ground my hips round and round, smearing our juices over the pink flesh between our lips. The folds of her pussy were swelling and so were mine as I rubbed our creases together, moaning and rocking and lost in the pleasure of it.

It was like riding a slow cresting wave, surfing it higher and higher as the sensation rose, making us both breathless. There was no hurrying it, no fast solution, just that gentle rubbing of our flesh, the friction building at its own slow, sweet pace.

Doc's hand moved over his cock. I felt it against my hip, but I couldn't even look. I bit my lip, watching her face as Mrs. B got there moments before I did, her orgasm trembling through her. The most amazing thing, the most wondrous and glorious thing, was feeling the flutter of her pussy against mine, clenching and releasing as she came, bucking and grinding up against me.

"Yes!" I groaned, rolling, rocking, sending myself right after her, my pussy spasming in delicious, shuddering waves, making me weak again. Doc grabbed onto me, holding my trembling shoulders as I moaned and shook with the force of it. He turned my face and kissed me, then, sucking my tongue into his mouth, his fingers slipping between our lips, rubbing through our wetness. He made me shiver when he brushed my still-pulsing clit.

"Which one of us do you want?" Mrs. B smiled up at him.

"Both of you." He helped me down off of Mrs. B. I wasn't sure my legs would hold me and I leaned forward onto the towel on the counter between Mrs. B's legs, still panting. "At once, preferably."

She laughed, a low, throaty sound. "Greedy Doc."

I found myself looking at Mrs. B's pussy, glistening now with our juices, as Doc grabbed my hips.

"Or maybe just Ronnie." He moved his fingers through my slit. I gasped when his fingers found me. "Bent over a different counter this time."

"Easy!" I winced when his cock found me, following the path his fingers had taken through my slick, swollen folds. "Please, Doc."

"Promise." He groaned when he moved forward and up, one hand moving around to my belly, the other massaging my ass.

He went slow, giving me easy half-strokes, rocking me forward toward Mrs. B. I rested my cheek on her thigh as he fucked me and she stroked my hair, still wet from the shower. The hand on my belly moved a little lower, massaging as it went, his fingers finally reaching the top of my slit, moving the swell of my lips against my clit with the motion. It made me tingle.

"Do you like that tight little nineteen-year-old cunt, Doc?" Mrs. B asked and I felt my ass and pussy clench at her words.

He groaned, his fingers slipping further between my cleft, finding my clit, making me gasp.

"So tight and sweet." She stroked my hair. I looked up at her and saw that she was smiling down at me. "You have a beautiful cunt, baby."

Doc thrust harder now, but I didn't complain because his fingers rubbed me, the sensation almost too much to bear.

"So do you, Mrs. B." My eyes moved over the glistening folds, seeing a little pink peeking out between. I leaned in and kissed it, just a light kiss, but she moaned, rocking her hips forward a little.

I slipped my tongue into it then, sending a shudder through her, and then I was lost in her pussy, sinking into it with a moan as Doc pushed a little deeper now, his fingers still working my clit.

"Good girl," Mrs. B murmured as I parted her fat lips with my tongue, pushing against the hood of her clit, rolling it around. She tasted a little different and I realized that it was the taste of us together, a light musky scent filling my nose as I moved my head and mouth from side to side against her flesh.

Doc slipped out of my pussy, rubbing the head along my slit, meeting his fingers at my clit. I moaned against Mrs. B's flesh as he rocked the spongy tip there for a while, pressing it into me with his fingers. It made me suck and lap at her even more, urgent and a little wild, and she cried out, digging her nails into my shoulders.

"Oh fuck!" She grabbed my head, guiding me, smashing my lips and tongue against her clit as she came again, the spasms sending her legs straight out, trembling with the force of her orgasm.

She whispered as she loosened her grip in my hair. "Oh God... oh, baby... you have the sweetest tongue."

I moved up her body, feeling Doc's shaft slip from between my legs as I kissed her, the taste of her between us, filling our mouths. He nudged me from behind, his hands running down my ribcage, my hips.

"Turn around." He twisted my pelvis with his hands, grabbing me and putting me up onto the counter in front of Mrs. B. He pressed my knees back, opening me up completely, and Mrs. B grabbed them from behind, holding them open.

"Fuck her." Mrs. B's words were whispered into my ear, but she was looking at Doc. "Make her cum all over that big, fat cock."

I groaned as Doc slid back inside of me and we started rocking, Mrs. B still holding onto my knees, keeping me spread wide for him. The only sound was the wet music of my pussy being pounded and our breath, everything coming faster and faster. Mrs. B's breasts were a full, soft cushion behind me, her body smooth against mine.

"Do you like that cock, baby?" Mrs. B whispered in my ear, sliding both hands along the insides of my thighs, squeezing them, making me moan.

"Yes!" I looked down at him disappearing into my pussy. He was sinking all the way into me, working hard, and I had forgotten that I was sore—I wasn't sore in that moment. My pussy was on fire, throbbing and aching for more. I just couldn't get enough.

I didn't need any prompting this time, I met Doc's eyes and told him, "Fuck me, Doc. Fuck me hard! I want it hard! Please! Please!"

I wanted to feel every part of him inside of me, and I clawed and clutched at his arms as he grabbed my hips and drove harder, groaning as he did, his cock swelling inside of me.

Mrs. B moaned in my ear. "That's it, baby. Take that big cock. Let him fuck you until you cum."

When his thumb moved over my clit, that's just what I did, my swollen, wet pussy getting its aching release, squeezing his cock and asking for more. I moaned and gripped the strong muscles in his upper arms as I came.

"Oh hell!" He groaned.

I felt the first burst of his cum as he began to withdraw. The second wave hit my clit and sent me into orbit and I was squirming and moaning in Mrs. B's arms. His cock surged up over my belly, filling my navel with white hot fluid that dripped back down in rivers toward my swollen pussy.

He leaned forward to kiss me and then he kissed Mrs. B and then me again like he couldn't decide which of us he wanted to kiss more. I reached my hand down and rubbed his cum into my belly, over my mound, smiling.

"I need another bath!" I giggled.

"A tongue bath, maybe." Mrs. B chuckled.

Doc stood, letting out a deep breath. "Well whatever we do, it better be quick. I've got to get Janie and Henry in an hour."

I started. I had almost forgotten the whole reason I was in Key West with the Baumgartners in the first place. The thought of Janie and Henry made me flush.

It was a fast, cold dose of reality. *What are we doing?* "Are you ok?" Doc lifted my chin. It was the same question he had asked me last night, and I still didn't know the answer.

I just smiled at him and nodded.

Chapter Twelve

I started out hating Gretchen, the Super-Nanny, but what happened with Henry finally swayed me. No one could get that kid to go to sleep without a nightlight, and he was almost nine years old. Gretchen lived up to the nickname I had secretly given her when the Baumgartners and the Holmes decided to go out and leave us with all four kids.

Gretchen and I spent the whole day together talking, in between band-aids and peanut butter and jelly sandwiches, and while I didn't want to like her at first, eventually I found myself warming to her. I knew I was just jealous. She was beautiful, five years older than me, had been a nanny since she was my age, and was clearly more experienced and worldly than I was in a million different ways.

We lay out on the beach together and watched the kids play in the sand. She borrowed one of Mrs. B's bikinis, and I noticed she didn't have any problems down there about anything showing, and I got to wondering if she was shaved. She was whiter-blonde than Mrs. B, her hair straight and long instead of curly, her eyes an unusual green.

And Gretchen had a beautiful body that I couldn't help noticing—she was taller than me, with longer legs, fuller breasts, although more pale, I noticed, with a little satisfaction. Still, her skin was creamy and smooth and unmarked, and felt like velvet when I helped her put lotion all over her back.

I was quiet around her—but I was quiet a lot around new people. That didn't seem to matter to her, though. She talked about everything, non-stop.

"So how long are you guys staying in the Keys?" she asked.

"Another couple days." The thought made me sad.

"Don't you dread going back?" She shaded her eyes, sitting up on her elbow to look at the kids. "Although if I had something to go back to, it might be more appealing. No boyfriend... not even a girlfriend."

I swallowed hard when she winked over at me. "How about you?"

"No." I watched her cross her ankles. Her toes were painted pink. "No boyfriend here either..."

"Sounds like we both need to get laid!"

I didn't reply, but God, something curled in my belly when she talked like that and I sat and watched the tops of her glistening breasts rising and falling with her breath.

I wanted to tell her about the Baumgartners, but I just couldn't bring myself to. She kept asking me lots of questions about my sex life—it seemed like that's what she wanted to talk about, mostly.

I couldn't answer any of her questions honestly. The last man I slept with? *Doc.* Had I ever been with a woman? *Mrs. B!* Had I ever used a vibrator? *Yes. Mrs. B's!* It just seemed safer to not say anything at all.

Still, together, we had a good day, and pretty much did everything we could think of to wear the kids out, between swimming, taking them for a long walk to go get ice cream, and then playing flashlight tag on the beach before bed. I still figured they'd be up giggling and talking like I used to do on sleepovers, but Janie could barely brush her teeth because she was yawning so much and the Holmes kids were zonked out already in my bed.

Then Henry started having a fit because the little bulb in his nightlight had burnt out and all I could find were empty packages in the drawers—we were all out.

"I'll leave the hall light on and the door cracked open," I offered in an attempt to get him to stop wailing.

"It won't work!" came the muffled cry from his pillow. "The monsters will come!"

I shrugged my shoulders at Gretchen, who cocked her head and pursed her lips and then headed down the stairs. I attempted to calm Henry.

"You know there aren't any monsters." I squatted next to his bed.

"Yes there are!" He turned his tear-streaked face to me.

"Of course there are." Gretchen stood in the doorway. I looked up to see her carrying a spray bottle from under the kitchen sink that I recognized as the one that Mrs. B used to mist the plants. "That's why you need Monster Spray." Both Henry and I stared at her, open-mouthed.

"Monster Spray?" Henry sounded doubtful as he sat up and looked at her from his bed.

Gretchen brought it over and set it on the night table. "That's right. I always carry some in my purse, just in case. I filled this spray bottle with it."

I couldn't tell if he was buying it or not, but at least he was quiet. "Does it really work?"

"Of course!" Gretchen knelt by his bed, picking up the bottle. "If you see or hear a monster, all you have to do it spray it and it will run right away!"

She hit the trigger and misted the air, showing him.

"Cool!" His eyes lit up and he reached for the spray bottle. Then he frowned. "It's not just water?"

"Smell it." She stood and folded her arms across her chest.

He sniffed the nozzle. "Ew!"

"Told you." Gretchen smiled, tucking a long piece of blonde hair behind her ears. "Monster Spray. 100% guaranteed."

He grinned at her. "Cool! Good night."

With that, he put the spray bottle on the night table, laid down and closed his eyes. I stared at her, incredulous. That's when I knew I really liked her.

As we headed down the stairs, I asked, "What was in it?"

"Vinegar and water."

I laughed, shaking my head in amazement. Gretchen was spending the night with us, too, since Mr. and Mrs. Holmes said they'd probably be out at least until 2 a.m. We had the sofa bed pulled out in the living room and she and I curled up on it with a bowl of microwave popcorn between us and put in the first non-kid movie I'd watched in weeks, *Tristan and Isolde.* When it was over and our popcorn bowl was empty, Gretchen grabbed the remote and turned off the TV with a sigh.

"Well that sucked." She lay back on her pillow with a groan. "But that Tristan... God, what a hottie!"

I made a face. "I would have stayed with Lord Marke if I were her."

She smiled over at me, raising her eyebrows. "Someone likes older guys, huh?" I didn't say anything, I just grabbed a half-popped kernel from the bottom of the bowl and crunched it between my teeth.

"Doc is a hottie." She narrowed her eyes at me like a cat. In this light, they almost glowed like a cat's eyes. "Don't you think?" I couldn't help smiling and nodding.

"I'd let him get into my panties." She rolled toward the bowl and fished for half-popped kernels, too. "I bet he's got a nice big cock."

"Gretchen!" I looked around like someone could hear us.

Her words made my ass clench and my heart beat a little faster. After talking about sex all day, now lying in bed with her in nothing but our t-shirts and panties, I couldn't help but be a little turned-on.

She grinned, her long, blonde hair swaying like a curtain. "I'm just saying."

"He does." I lowered my voice, meeting her wide-eyes. I couldn't stand it anymore. I had to tell her *something!*

She squealed, sitting up and grabbing my wrists. "Oh my God! You have to tell me!"

Now that I'd said that much, I wasn't sure I wanted to say any more. I put the popcorn bowl on the end table and took a drink of my Coke, stalling. When I turned back to her, she was obviously waiting and I knew I had to say something.

"I saw them having sex," I admitted, feeling my blush now.

"And?" She put her hands behind her head, the white t-shirt she was wearing pulling up to reveal a pair of pink panties.

"You're right." I shrugged. I could picture his cock, could almost see and smell and taste it. It made me ache just imagining it. "He's... pretty big."

She sighed, frowning. "That's no fun! Give me details. I haven't been laid since I took this job. Believe me, I'm dying for details!"

I stretched out, leaning on my elbow and propping my head in my hand, remembering that first night I had seen Doc and Mrs. B. having sex.

"I got up to go to the bathroom." I closed my eyes, picturing them before going on. "And I heard them... Mrs. B was... moaning..."

Gretchen's eyes brightened. "Uh-huh."

I shifted on the bed, getting tingly just remembering it. "And I noticed their door was open a little. I could see them in the mirror."

She shifted, too, her thighs clenching. "And?"

"Mrs. B was on her knees... she had him in her mouth," I said. "But when she stopped for a minute, I could see his...cock. It was pretty big."

She made a soft sound in her throat. "Show me. With your hands."

I did and she groaned again.

"God, I miss it." She sighed, her hands resting on her belly now. "So what else did you see?"

I decided not to mention the part where they were talking about me. "He turned her around and bent her over, so she was on her hands and knees."

Gretchen sighed, her eyes closing. "Mmmm."

"And Mrs. B was saying things like..." I hesitated, swallowing as I watched Gretchen's hand moving up toward her breast. She was just nudging it a little, moving it under her t-shirt, shifting on the bed.

"Go on," she urged, her eyes still closed.

"Like... I want you to fuck me... put it in my... cunt..."

Gretchen moaned when I said that, a real moan. "Oh, Ronnie, I'm so horny I can't stand it."

I nodded, but I knew she couldn't see me. Telling her, remembering, watching how flushed she was getting and how her nipples were starting to stand up under her t-shirt was making me wet, too.

"Then he started fucking her," I went on, my voice getting lower, a little more husky. "From behind like that. Grabbing her hips and just slamming into her."

She let out a long breath, her hand moving between her legs, cupping herself through her panties, squeezing her legs together. Again, I wondered if she was shaved.

"And she was moaning and fucking him back." My voice was almost a whisper now. "Saying, 'Oh, Doc, fuck me hard, baby. Make me cum!" I did Mrs. B's voice as best I could, making Gretchen shiver, her hand moving slowly over her panties, now.

"But the best part," I whispered, slipping my hand down between my own legs. The crotch of my panties was damp under my t-shirt. "Was after she came all over that big, hard cock..."

Gretchen's breath was coming faster, her fingers brushing over her panties, her other hand cupping her breast. I could see her finger moving, barely noticeable, over her nipple.

"He pulled out of her pussy." I closed my eyes and remembered how slick his cock was with her juices as I rubbed myself. "And put it into her mouth, and made her swallow all his hot cum."

Gretchen gasped and I opened my eyes to see her looking at me, her gaze shifting between my legs where I was cupping my mound.

"Don't stop!" She groaned. "God, I love the taste of cum. I'd love to taste him."

I felt my belly flutter when she said that, remembering how Doc tasted shooting his cum into my mouth, swallowing and swallowing it.

"Did you play with yourself?" she asked me, her eyes back on mine.

I nodded, my fingers rubbing the growing wet spot on my panties. "I couldn't help it."

"I don't blame you." Her eyes were closed again, but she hadn't stopped rubbing between her legs. "I don't know how you can be around him and not want to fuck him."

I wanted to tell her, but I didn't know how.

Then she said, "And Mrs. B isn't bad, either."

I felt my pussy twinge. "She's beautiful."

"Did they know you were there?"

I shook my head, lying. "No."

She opened her eyes and smiled at me. "Too bad. You might have had some more fun than just rubbing off, huh?"

I shrugged, biting my lip, my eyes dipping back down to her pink panties. She was moving her fingers in little circles in one spot.

"God, I want a cock in me," she murmured, and as I watched, she slipped her hand under the top band of her panties. "Don't you ever fantasize about Doc fucking you?"

I tried to control how fast my breath was coming now, but I couldn't help rubbing myself.

"Yes," I admitted. Then I had an idea. "You know... Mrs. B has a vibrator upstairs. And Doc has a porn video."

Gretchen opened her eyes, smiling. "Now we're talking! Where?"

"Their room." I watched her fingers moving under her panties. It was making me dizzy with lust, and I kept remembering the taste of Mrs. B in my throat.

"Let's go!" She hopped off the bed and headed for the stairs.

I followed her, not quite believing we were doing this, but so turned on by now that I didn't care. It felt naughty, and somehow that made it even more exciting.

When I showed her the vibrator, she grinned and took it from me, turning it on full blast. "Oh, God... If the Holmes weren't Mr. and Mrs. Baptist and I wasn't too afraid I'd get fired, I'd have one of these in every color."

I found the porn video that Doc had been watching inside of the DVD player in their room.

"*The Babysitter Learns a Lesson?*" Gretchen read the title on the box and looked up at me with a smile. "Gee, you think Doc fantasizes about you, too?"

I just shrugged, turning on the TV and hitting play. We settled on the Baumgartner's bed just like we had downstairs, only this time there was a big black vibrator between us instead of a bowl of popcorn and the people on the screen were most definitely not Tristan and Isolde.

It was the same couple, the older guy, the young girl in pigtails with her lollipop. Gretchen was watching it, but I was just listening and watching her face, her reactions. It got to the part where the girl was rubbing her pussy with the lollipop, and Gretchen pulled her panties down her thighs. I wanted to get a closer look but was afraid to.

I heard her fingers moving in and out, rubbing through her wetness. I took my panties off, too, tossing them with hers, a little pile of pink and white. On the screen, the older man was about to put his cock into the girl's ass. That was the part, I remembered, that had shocked me so much I gasped out loud, and then Doc had seen me touching myself on the stairs. My pussy ached at the memory and I looked over at Gretchen, her eyes glued to the screen.

"Mmmm…" She watched him press his cock against her ass. "God, I miss that."

I stared at her, my fingers stopping their little circles against my clit. "Have you—?"

She glanced over at me, noticing for the first time, I think, that my panties were off and I was playing, too.

"Oh yeah." She gave me a wicked little grin. "I love having a cock in my ass."

The thought seemed so foreign to me, so... naughty and wrong. But the girl on the screen seemed to like it a lot. She was moaning and saying, "Fuck my ass with that big cock!"

"Can I go first?" Gretchen picked up the vibrator.

I nodded, watching her turn it on, just the sound of it sending shivers through me. She slid it down between her legs, rubbing the head through her slit, moaning. Her other hand went under her shirt, and I could see her playing with her nipple. I longed to pull up her shirt and see it.

"Oh yeah," she whispered as she slipped the vibrator inside of her.

I sat up on my elbow a little, looking down between her legs. There was a small landing strip of light blonde hair leading down to her pussy, but her lips were shaved smooth and were glistening wet. I fingered myself as I watched her, the thick length of the cock disappearing and then reappearing, slick with her juices.

She was still watching the screen and I glanced over at it again. Now it was the girl and the older guy and his wife. The wife was licking the girl's pussy on the bed, and the older man was behind his wife, fucking her that way. Gretchen turned the vibrator up a notch, moaning and fucking herself faster.

My pussy was throbbing, my clit humming under my fingers. I pulled up my shirt, playing with my nipples, too, turning the hum to a deep, delicious buzz. I moaned, rocking on the bed, and Gretchen looked over at me, her eyes half-closed.

"Feel good?" Her gaze was between my legs. I spread myself a little more open, tilting my hips so she could see. Her tongue moved over her lower lip as she watched me, the vibrator speeding up even faster.

"Want to know what feels better?" I took my fingers out of my pussy and licked them. She raised her eyebrows in surprise but her eyes never left my tongue moving over the tips of my fingers.

"What?" she whispered. I didn't answer but instead I slipped between her legs, my mouth moving right over her pussy, sucking on her clit.

"Oh!" she cried, surprised at first, but I took the vibrator from her hands, moving it, twisting it in and out of her pussy as I licked her. "Ohhhhhhh! Oh yessss!"

She opened her eyes to look down at me, her long, straight blonde hair framing her face, her eyes dazed with pleasure. I reached up, tugging at her shirt, pushing it up above her breasts. They were a little fuller than mine, her nipples pink and thick and round in the middle of a rosy areola. I rolled one between my finger and thumb, feeling her jump.

I flicked my tongue over and over her clit, which was fat and swollen with a thick hood. She tasted different from Mrs. B, or even me, slightly more musky and a little tart, but she was soaking wet, so slippery that the vibrator slid easily in and out of her pussy as I fucked her.

"Oh sweet Jesus!" She moaned, her head going back, her hips moving up, giving in completely. I slid the vibrator out of her pussy and heard her groan, but I replaced it with my fingers, two of them, remembering what Doc had done to me the other night on the counter. I crooked my fingers, feeling her jump and wiggle at my touch.

The vibrator was still going so I took it in my other hand and pressed the head to the top of her slit, right where those light blonde hairs began to curl, still moving my tongue back and forth over her clit. She really seemed to like that, bucking up and tugging at her own nipples. They were as red as little cherries now with her twisting and pulling on them.

I wished I had three hands because my pussy was aching to be touched. I imagined what it would be like if Doc walked in and saw us. I wanted his cock inside of me, pumping me full of his hard, hot flesh. Gretchen began thrashing as I rubbed deep inside her pussy, feeling something swelling under my fingers. Her flesh was so wet, I could barely keep her in my mouth and her juices ran down my chin and over her ass.

"Oh wait!" Her hands pushed at me as I pressed even harder inside, stretching the smooth walls of her pussy with my fingers again and again. "Oh, God, wait, what—?"

And then she was coming, her cries loud and high, almost little squeaks as she trembled all over with pleasure. Gasping, she grabbed my head, pressing it to her mound, mashing my face there.

"Don't stop," she begged. "Lick me, oh yeah, more, more!"

I did, taking the vibrator and sliding it down between my own legs, rubbing it over my clit as I let her use my tongue. Her hips were rocking and grinding into my face and I just opened my mouth and stuck out my tongue for her.

"Oh my fucking God!" She moaned, her dazed eyes looking down at me between her legs. I saw her gaze flicker to the screen behind me and I could hear the movie still going, the sounds of fucking, moaning, swearing, panting. It was nothing compared to what was happening on the Baumgartner's bed between me and Gretchen.

My clit found the edge of the vibrator's shaft, that big black cock nestled between my legs as I ate her pussy for everything I was worth. The sounds of her pleasure made me dizzy. It was like feeding an addiction—I just wanted more and more. My pussy was so swollen and slick, throbbing for release, and I rocked my hips against the cock between my thighs, working toward it.

"Make me come!" She panted, her smooth, pale belly undulating as she rocked. "Please, please make me come!

I groaned, pushing myself to my own climax as I moved my tongue faster and faster against her pussy, not knowing where I started and she began. I came so hard I couldn't even see straight and my ears were ringing and all I could do was lick and swallow her as she came too, her soft cries filling the room.

"Holy shit," she whispered as I sat up between her thighs, wiping my face with the back of my hand. It didn't do much good, I was literally just soaked with her all the way down to my nipples. I grinned, still breathless and she smiled back at me, looking dazed. There was a huge wet spot on the bed, too, that I wondered how were going to hide.

Then we heard Henry screaming, "Monster! There's a monster!"

Gretchen pulled her t-shirt down, grabbing her panties. "I'll get him. You...clean up."

I turned off the movie, put everything back, and put my own panties back on. Then I washed up. By the time I was done, Henry was back to sleep and Gretchen was downstairs under the covers.

"Are you asleep?" I whispered, climbing in with her.

We were sharing the sofa bed tonight. She didn't answer me, and I could hear her breathing was deep and even. Either she was sleeping or pretending to be. I closed my eyes, feeling a slow heat burning in my chest as I remembered what we'd done. I snuggled up to her back, drifting off, still tasting her in my mouth.

Chapter Thirteen

Janie crept in between Gretchen and I on the sofa bed at what felt like it had to be five in the morning. It was full light, though, so I knew it couldn't be. She snuggled up to me and I kissed her cheek, pulling her close and trying to fall back asleep, but I couldn't. I kept remembering the night before.

Gretchen was still sleeping, her blonde hair like gold strands falling around her face and shoulders, her lips a perfect little rosebud. She had such soft, delicate features, like a doll. I was both envious and attracted at the same time, a paradox that made me squirmy.

Janie noticed I wasn't sleeping and she turned in my arms. "I'm hungry."

"What time is it?" I whispered back.

"Eight, I think." She snuggled closer.

She was getting big to be doing this—almost ten—caught right between that place of being a little girl and not quite a teenager, the lost land of "tween." I looked at her and remembered how little she had been when I first started babysitting for them. She was growing up, and starting to look more and more like her beautiful mother every day. I found myself envious of her, too, and almost wished I could go back there to those pre-teen days myself, when things didn't seem and feel so complicated.

"Want pancakes?" I smiled and tucked a honey-colored curl behind her ear.

"Special?" She perked up, her voice getting high and louder, making Gretchen sigh and shift in her sleep. I noticed the covers pull over the swell of her behind and it made my belly tighten.

"Yep." I yawned. "Go tell Henry, and see if Noah and Sarah want any."

Janie scrambled off the sofa bed to go wake Henry and the Holmes kids and I got up and tugged a pair of shorts on that I'd left on the floor next to me. Gretchen rolled over fully onto her belly, the covers shifting and showing her panties—the pink ones—and the tops of her creamy white thighs. I wanted to kiss her there and resisted the impulse.

I had three pancakes done before they all finally tumbled down the stairs and ran into the kitchen. Janie was explaining what "Ronnie's Special Pancakes" were to Noah and Sarah as they sat down at the table.

"They're *HUGE* pancakes, all rolled up with applesauce inside and whipped cream on top," she said, making her hands into a circle the size of a dinner plate for emphasis.

"And cinnamon sugar." Henry dipped his finger into the whipped cream on the way by. "Don't forget that. It's my favorite part."

"Ronnie's Special Pancakes." I was just finishing the last one. I gave them each a plate with one pancake each, plus a fork and a glass of milk.

"Mmmm, looks good you guys." Gretchen stretched sleepily from the doorway. I saw her standing there, still in her t-shirt and panties. She raised her eyebrows at me with a grin. "They're going to be high on sugar all day."

I shrugged, my eyes moving down her long, bare legs. "It's a treat."

"It sure is." Doc came in behind Gretchen, looking at her in t-shirt and panties, though, and not at the pancakes I'd made. "Did you sleep well, Gretchen?"

"Ronnie hogs the covers." She laughed. "But besides that, fine. I could use some coffee."

"Me, too." He glanced briefly at me. "Can you put coffee on, Ronnie?"

"I'll help." Gretchen came to stand next to me, rubbing her hip against mine as she turned on the coffee maker, putting in a filter for me to dole out scoops into. It didn't take both of us to make coffee, and Doc was watching, his eyes sharp, noticing the way she slipped her hand over the small of my back.

Gretchen went back to the table, smiling at Doc as she stole some of the whipped cream from the top of Sarah's pancake. "So, Doc, you were telling me before... you have a motorcycle back home?"

Doc's eyes were on her mouth as she sucked whipped cream off her finger and so were mine. "Harley Electra Glide."

"Really?" Her eyes widened for a moment and then softened as she rubbed her lips with her wet finger. "I would so love to go for a ride with you. Wouldn't you like to take a ride with Doc, Ronnie?"

I swallowed, seeing her eyes moving over me, and I glanced at Doc, who was smiling, looking a little amused.

He leaned back in his chair, his eyes dipping down to her lap where her t-shirt was pulled up, exposing her bare thighs and pink panties. My eyes went there, too. "Gimme a call when we get back. I can definitely take you both for a ride."

She smiled over at me. "Motorcycles are so sexy...don't you think so, Ronnie?"

"Yummy." I grabbed coffee mugs out of the cupboard. I poured coffee for the three of us, putting full cups in front of each of them. The kids were wolfing down their pancakes, none of them even speaking.

"Do you have cream and sugar?" Gretchen looked up at me. "Can't have it without cream and sugar."

Her eyes met mine and the look in them stopped me.

"I love cream and sugar." My voice was smooth and low when I replied.

Doc cocked his head at me. "I thought you drank your coffee black?"

I shrugged, standing. "Sometimes a girl likes cream and sugar, what can I say?"

"Done!" Henry exclaimed, as if it had been a contest, his face full of applesauce and whipped cream. "Who wants to play Tomb Raider?"

"Me!" Noah said through a mouthful of pancake. He wasn't even half done. I put the cream and sugar on the table in front of Gretchen and her smile warmed me to my toes.

"Thanks." Her eyes were even warmer than her smile. Doc looked between us, his face bemused. Janie and Sarah followed the boys and the luring call of video games into the living room. I sat next to Gretchen with my own cup of coffee, feeling her hand sliding over my thigh under the table.

"I'm going to take a shower." Doc stretched, still wearing that bemused smile. "I'll leave you two girls alone."

* * * *

Mrs. Holmes came to collect Gretchen and the kids just before dinner and we spent every moment together until then. I told Mrs. B I wasn't hungry and went to my room after they left. I couldn't get Gretchen out of my head.

Janie came in to say good night and we snuggled and talked for a minute before she went to bed.

"I love Gretchen," she sighed. "I hope I grow up to look like her."

I smiled, but I knew what she meant. Gretchen couldn't help but leave an impression. "You'll be beautiful, Janie, and you'll look like you."

"I wish my mom and dad would get an *au pair*." She pulled her arm around me tighter and snuggled close. "They keep talking about it."

"Really?" I knew how much the Holmes' were paying Gretchen, because she told me. I didn't know if the Baumgartners could afford her, in spite of Doc's salary and Mrs. B's side business. Me, though, I was free—at least on this trip. "Well, maybe some day."

"Janie!" Mrs. B called. "Bed!"

"Goodnight." Janie kissed my cheek.

"'Night, sweetie."

She shut my door and I curled up to read for a while, but I couldn't really concentrate. I kept remembering last night, being with Gretchen, how warm and soft and open she was, how we rode that sexual tension all through the day until I was stretched so taut I felt like I was going to burst.

"Ronnie?" It was Doc, knocking at my door.

"Come in."

He came and sat on the edge of my bed. "You want to talk about it?"

Rolling to my back, I looked up at him. "About what?"

He grinned. "Oh, I don't know... Super-Nanny and her magical pink underwear?"

I laughed. "I assume you mean Gretchen?"

"What happened last night? Something, obviously..."

I flushed. "Why do you say that?"

He raised his eyebrows. "Because your feet haven't touched the ground all day."

I couldn't help smiling. "Ok... so... something happened."

"Something good?"

"Yes... very good..." I squirmed, remembering. Glancing up at him, I frowned. "You're not mad?"

"No, of course not." He smiled. "We just want you to be happy, Ronnie."

He chucked me under the chin, but his hand stayed there, slipping lower down my neck, drawing patterns over my chest at the top edge of my tank-tee. "Do *we* still make you happy?"

I beamed up at him. "Oh, yes!"

He chuckled. "Well, then, would you like to come to bed?"

I hesitated as his fingers played with my spaghetti straps, looking at him in his boxer-briefs. "Your bed?"

"Carrie's already in it." His finger followed the line of the strap down over the material, running directly into my nipple. It was soft, but started to harden the minute he touched it. "And she's waiting for us."

I went with him. I couldn't help myself. The thought of listening to them on the other side of the wall, the headboard, the squeak of the bed, her moans, and not being a part of it, was too much. I had to go.

Mrs. B flipped channels on the TV when I came in, wearing just a t-shirt. She smiled, holding out her hand to me and I snuggled against her softness. It felt so good to be held.

"I hate summer." She sighed. "Nothing but re-runs and Reality TV. Have you seen this *Nanny 911* show?" I shook my head as she paused there, screaming kids running around the screen, hitting their parents, throwing things.

"They could take a lesson from you, that's for sure." She kissed the top of my head. Doc smiled as he climbed into bed on her other side. I knew she was just petting me—but it felt good. I liked being petted. She turned the TV off with a sigh, tossing the remote on the bed. "So much for that. We've got better things to do, hm?"

I nodded against her breast, already feeling warm. She tilted my face up to hers, kissing me. She tasted salty and I wondered what they had for dinner. I didn't have any more time to think, though, because she kissed me down to the bed, her hand moving up under my shirt, rubbing and squeezing my breast.

She rolled onto me, her thighs soft and smooth against mine, and I took the gentle weight of her, my hands moving under her shirt in back, up over the rounded globes of her ass. We kissed like that for a long time, our lips meshing, our tongues entwined, until I could feel that sweet tingling all through my body, even in my toes and fingertips.

Then she sat up, straddling me, pulling her t-shirt over her head. I watched her revealing her body, my eyes lost in her sloping curves, her golden skin. I reached for her breasts, my hands seeming so small as I tried to cup them, hold them. She leaned forward, over me, and I pressed my face against them, her nipples hardening under my mouth.

I drowned myself in Mrs. B's flesh, running my tongue from side to side, first one nipple, then the other. She held herself above me, the heat of her pussy pressed against my tummy, watching me with half-closed eyes. I saw Doc stretched out beside us, his cock hard in his fist. I remembered estimating for Gretchen with my hands how big he was, but I think I didn't quite give him enough length. It seemed bigger now to me as he pumped it through his fist.

Mrs. B moved, sliding her hips up, grabbing the headboard. She came up and put a knee on either side of my head, wiggling a little as she positioned herself. I looked at her for a moment, her skin so smooth, showing a little pink inside as she spread her thighs. It was wetter in there, I could see it, and I could smell her, that sweet musk that made my pussy twinge and pulse.

I opened her up with my tongue, starting at the top of her cleft, moving it from side to side, teasing her clit for a moment before searching lower, trying to find the source of her honey. I groaned when I reached it, that little hole that was already seeping fluid onto my tongue. Probing there, making my tongue hard, I grabbed her hips, pushing it in as far as it would go.

"Oh!" Mrs. B gasped as I fucked her with my tongue, swallowing as much of her as I could, my nose pressed hard against her clit. I was squeezing my thighs together, feeling my own pussy aching, as I slid my tongue back up, making it a little cup and taking her juices with me, spreading them all over her clit, making it even more slick.

"Oh yes," she murmured as I poked and prodded and pushed the hood back and touched the source of her pleasure directly. I slid my hand down between my legs, shoving it down under the elastic band, seeking my own heat. I was swollen and slippery wet already and I moaned into her pussy as I started to rub my clit.

I felt Doc's hands, then, pulling at my shorts, my panties, peeling them off. His tongue was between my legs, licking and sucking as he slipped his fingers up inside me. I moaned into her pussy as she rocked on me, working her pink flesh against the soft wetness of my tongue. I couldn't swallow all of her, and I could feel her juices pooling at the hollow of my throat.

Doc pushed my legs back with his palms, his face buried between my thighs, licking me until I couldn't concentrate on anything, including Mrs. B. She rocked and rocked, holding onto the headboard, her moans low and long as she ground herself against me.

"Beautiful." Doc murmured, his tongue on me again, flicking faster, sending waves of pleasure through me. His fingers were petting the entrance to my pussy, not sliding inside, just circling around and around the hole, making me squirm and moan.

Mrs. B's movements increased, her hips rolling faster, her moans louder, and I could see the slope of her belly, the curve of her breasts as they pressed against the headboard, her head going back as she used my tongue, her long hair brushing my breasts, making me shiver.

"Oh baby," she whispered. "Oh yes, sweetie, I'm gonna commmmmme!"

The last word turned into a long, sustained "mmmmm" and I moaned, licking her faster, feeling the pulse jump between my legs as Doc used his mouth on me, his fingers sliding through my slit. Mrs. B was shuddering and quaking with her climax, gripping the headboard and rocking, making it pound against the wall as she came.

Doc's tongue made fast circles over my clit, and I felt that familiar tug in my belly, something coiled there, waiting. Mrs. B moved off me, coming to snuggle next to me, but Doc didn't stop, and I looked down to see him, his eyes on mine, his mouth working.

I groaned when Mrs. B began to suck at my nipple, sending an immediate rush of heat to my pussy. Gasping, I grabbed for something to hold onto, finding Mrs. B's thigh, digging my fingers into her flesh.

"Don't stop," I begged, her fingers rubbing and pulling at my other nipple. "Ohhhhh God, pleeeease!"

I was so close, teetering right at the edge, and I felt Doc's fingers slip even lower, gently stroking the entrance to my ass. I gasped, my fingers tightening on Mrs. B's thigh as he slid one finger into that tight, puckered hole, his tongue still moving like lightning over my clit.

"Oh, no!" I begged, shaking my head, but it felt so good, the skin there incredibly sensitive as he moved just the tip of his finger there, in and out. "Oh God, I can't stand it!"

And I couldn't, it was too much—I came harder than I thought I could, violent spasms that shook my whole body, a white heat spreading through me in huge, throbbing waves. I put my arm over my eyes, panting, almost ashamed at my response. Mrs. B was kissing my shoulder and arm, and I felt Doc moving up to lie on the other side of me.

"Did you like that?" she whispered into my ear. "Didn't it feel good to have his finger in your ass?"

I moaned, peeking out at her, and whispered, "Yes."

"It's ok," she murmured. "I let him fuck my ass all the time."

I stared at her, remembering what Gretchen had said. *I love a cock in my ass.*

"Doesn't it hurt?"

She smiled. "Not if you do it right."

I looked over at Doc and then away. "It just... seems so... wrong... dirty..."

"That's part of what makes it fun," Doc whispered into my ear, making me shiver.

Mrs. B was tracing circles on my belly. "It's not, really. As long as you're clean."

I remembered in the bathtub, her pushing her finger into my ass.

"Does it..." I looked at her, frowning. "Does it feel good?"

She nodded. "Mmmm-hmm....God yes." Glancing over at Doc and some sort of communication seemed to pass between them. "Want to see?"

I felt my ass clench and I shook my head. "No!"

She chuckled, leaning in and kissing my cheek. "Not you... me."

"Oh." I glanced down, seeing that Doc was still at half-mast and standing up even straighter as Mrs. B knelt up, moving over me, kissing me.

"What—?" I started, but her mouth stopped me, her thighs pressing mine open under hers. Doc was moving behind her, I could see him above us.

"He has to lube everything up," she whispered against my cheek, resting her head on my shoulder. I could see that he had something in his hand, a tube, and he was squirting clear liquid into his hand.

"First he'll put it all over his cock..." I heard something slick, like the sound of his hand moving over his shaft.

"Then, he'll use his fingers... ohhhh..." Her body moved against mine, her back arching. I couldn't see what he was doing, but she told me. "He's putting his fingers in my ass, making it nice and slick."

"Does it hurt?"

"No." She shook her head against my shoulder. "Just have to relax... open up... mmmm... let him work it open with his fingers..."

"Ready, baby?" Doc murmured, and I could feel her hands tightening on my shoulders as she nodded her head.

"Yes." She hissed and closed her eyes for a moment. "Oh God... he's pressing the head of his cock in... that's the hardest part... just have to... ohhhhhh God, baby."

Doc groaned a little, his weight shifting on the bed. "It's okay, it's okay."

"Yes," she whispered again, loud enough for him to hear. "More... more..."

She kissed my cheek, my neck. "Ahhhh God... that's it, baby... I can take it... the head's almost in..." I couldn't tell who she was talking to anymore, him or me. "Deeper... oooohhhh yeahhh... deeper... mmmmmmm." She rocked back a little against him now, her breasts swaying against mine. "He's in me, now... his cock is in my ass..."

I looked up at her face, the expression caught somewhere between pleasure and pain. "All the way in?"

"Almost." She panted, groaning when he shoved into that last inch. She smiled at me, kissing me on the mouth, her tongue petting mine. I could feel him rocking her, fucking her, driving her forward onto me.

"Now comes the fun part," she whispered into my ear, pressing her breasts to mine. "Oooo God, that's gooood..."

She moaned and panted against my ear, rocking back against him. "Yes, baby, yes... fuck my ass!"

The sound of her words thrilled me, although I couldn't imagine his cock where it was, stretching her open...

"Want to see?" It was like she was reading my mind. She went fully up to her hands and knees. "Go on."

I wiggled out from under, crawling behind her as Doc grabbed her hips, pressing deep. His eyes were on me, watching me as I knelt up next to her.

"See." She showed me, spreading her cheeks wide.

I could see his shaft reappearing as he pulled back, the head popping under that tight, wrinkled hole. The lube he had used glistened and pooled against her flesh. In spite of my hesitation and my own fear, my pussy was aching and I watched, fascinated, as he began to move through that snug channel even faster, making Mrs. B moan louder.

Sliding my hand along the back of her thigh, I found her pussy, wet and swollen. She arched her back, rocking against my hand, his cock. His balls were slapping against her flesh now and she ground her hips back into him.

"That's it, baby!" She moaned against the bed. "Fuck that tight little asshole!"

I slid a finger into her, then two, pushing them all the way in. She gasped and panted, her breasts swaying under her, the nipples grazing their mattress. My thumb found her clit, rubbing it in circles and she cried, "Yes, oh yes!" when I started massaging it.

Kneeling up next to Doc, I watched him fuck her, his cock red and swollen, his eyes half closed, his breath coming faster and faster. I knew the sound of him growing close, now.

"I want to see you cum." I watched him drive deeper, harder. "Please."

He moaned, leaning in and kissing me, sucking my tongue into his mouth as he fucked her ass, that taut ring of flesh, never stopping. She was shaking, her thighs trembling, and I worked my hand faster, my fingers pressed deep into her, realizing I could actually feel his cock shoving into her through the thin membrane between the slick, smooth walls of her pussy and the humid tunnel of her ass.

"Doc!" She grunted and shoved back on him, and I knew she was coming. I knew the sound, the shudder and thrust of her, and I rubbed and rubbed her clit, sending her.

"Yeah, baby!" He groaned in response, pulling his cock out of her ass.

Without thinking, I grabbed it, pumping it in my fist over her ass. He held onto me as his hips bucked, his cum exploding over the small of her back. I pointed the head between her legs and watched as thick streams of hot, white fluid splashed over her now-gaping asshole, slipping down through her pussy lips in a rich, creamy river right down the center, aiming for her clit.

Mrs. B collapsed onto the bed, covered in his cum. I held his slick, softening cock in my hand and kissed him again.

"See?" Mrs. B murmured over her shoulder at me.

"Yes," I whispered against Doc's mouth with a shiver.

And I did.

Chapter Fourteen

I snuck back into my own room before it was light, so Janie and Henry wouldn't see me coming out of their mom and dad's room. Mrs. B pulled me back for a moment, kissing me on the mouth, putting a lazy, sleepy arm around my neck, making me want to stay.

I watched her turn and snuggle into Doc's back as I closed the door. He was snoring. I had a twinge of guilt thinking about all of it before I drifted back off to sleep, but our Key West vacation was over tomorrow. We were flying home and returning to our normal lives. I could help wondering—was this my "new normal?"

Janie and Henry arguing woke me up—at least, that's what I thought it was. By the time I grabbed myself a shower and went downstairs to scrounge a late breakfast, I found the Holmes' kids playing the X-Box with the Baumgartner's kids while Gretchen and Doc were sitting at the kitchen table. There was a box of Kleenex on it and Gretchen was blowing her nose. She looked awful and I went over to find out what had happened.

"They're firing me," Gretchen said as I took a seat across from Doc, not even looking up at me. "Guess what for?" I shook my head, throwing Doc a puzzled look. He just pulled another Kleenex out of the box and handed it to her.

"Condoms!" she hissed, looking over her shoulder to see if the kids were listening. They were glued to the X-Box.

I looked at Doc, incredulous. "What?"

"They're pretty fundamentally religious," Doc explained, handing her yet another Kleenex and she blew her nose loudly into it.

"I had them in my purse." Gretchen shook her head. "They fell out while I was looking for something and she saw them."

I leaned back in my chair, crossing my arms. "I don't get it."

"Maureen Holmes is a prude." Mrs. B came into the kitchen and poured herself a cup of coffee.

"Carrie," Doc warned, glancing toward the kids.

She came over to the table and sat next to me, rolling her eyes. "She is. To expect a twenty-four year old woman to be a virgin in this day and age?"

Gretchen sniffed. "To be fair, I did tell her when I was hired that I had recommitted myself—which was technically true—is true."

I stared at her, remembering everything she had said to me the other night. And aside from that—did being with a girl not count?

"I have them just in case." She wiped her eyes with the tissue. They were red and swollen. "The box was unopened. I tried to explain it to her, but she didn't care."

"I'm sorry, Gretchen." I shook my head.

I couldn't imagine working for people like the Holmes, but then, the Baumgartners were about as far from the Holmes as you could get and still be on the same planet, I thought.

"If there's anything we can do, just tell us." Mrs. B reached past me and touched Gretchen's hand.

"When do you leave?" Doc asked.

"Tonight," Gretchen sniffed. "I'm supposed to be taking the kids to buy souvenirs for their friends, but I just had to talk to someone."

"You did the right thing," Mrs. B reassured her, squeezing her hand.

"I should go. I have to get back." Gretchen blew her nose again and sniffed. "Ronnie, will you walk me out?"

I nodded, going with her to the door. The kids were still playing video games and we stood outside on the front porch. I couldn't help putting my arms around her and hugging her. She hugged me back and we rocked a little like that.

"I'm sorry." I didn't know what else to say.

"It's okay. I'll be okay." She drew a shaky breath. "I feel better already, just seeing you."

Then I really didn't know what to say, but I could feel a heat spreading from my belly all through my limbs. Somehow we were kissing, then, a hungry, urgent kiss, one that made me wish we were alone.

"Let's get together," she whispered into my ear. "When we get back? Go to... lunch... or something."

"Or something." I nodded. "Okay." Her eyes were still red and swollen and puffy and she still looked awful, and I'd never wanted anyone more.

"Sarah! Noah!" She opened the door. They burst out, full of tales of *Lara Croft: Tomb Raider*.

I waved at them from the porch as Gretchen hustled them into the car. I waved until the car disappeared around the corner and then I went and sat in the living room with Janie and Henry, who were still playing the X-Box.

"You guys want to go swimming?" I twirled one of Janie's blonde curls around my finger and thought about the way Gretchen's hair swung around her face. "It's our last day, we should do something fun out in the sun."

Doc came back into the room, smiling at me. "You just want to work on your tan."

I stuck my tongue out at him. "So?" I grabbed the edge of my shorts, pulling them aside. "It's working— see...tan lines!"

His eyes dipped to the bend in my thigh, following it inward. "Uh-huh, I see. Although thanks to Carrie's little bikini, not too many."

"Well, we've got a surprise for you." Mrs. B came in and turned off the TV.

Janie and Henry both groaned simultaneously. "Mom!"

Mrs. B rolled her eyes. "Fine, if you'd rather play some video game than swim with dolphins..."

I gasped and Janie squealed, clutching me. "Oh my God!" Janie cried. "Really? Oh my God! I love you!" I laughed as she screeched and pulled me to standing, jumping up and down.

Doc shook his head. "Who would have thought a bunch of big fish would be so exciting?"

"They're *mammals*, Dad!" Janie rolled her eyes at him.

Doc winked at me as Janie pulled me upstairs to get ready. "Mammals, huh? Who knew?"

* * * *

It was the best possible next-to-last day of our vacation that I could imagine, and it just kept getting better. We spent an hour swimming with dolphins, and Janie and I were both fascinated by their smooth, rubbery bodies, the way they actually came up to play with us. I couldn't get enough, and the trainers showed us how to hang onto them and go for a ride. It was like hanging onto a slippery bullet, and I came up sputtering and laughing, one of the dolphins lifting me from underneath.

We changed and went to dinner and the kids went to the game room and Mrs. B and I got out on the dance floor. The music was loud and it didn't matter what was playing, because it was just the beat we were rocking to, wild, like we didn't care who was watching. Doc was, though. I saw him out of the corner of my eye, leaning back and sipping a margarita.

I had three margaritas myself, although I wasn't supposed to be drinking at all. No one paid any attention, and I was so thirsty after coming off the dance floor that I kept drinking Mrs. B's and she just kept ordering more in all sorts of yummy flavors.

By the time we drove home, I was flying, and I put my arms up over my head when Doc put the top to the convertible down and me and Henry and Janie sat in the back and sang as loud as we could to whatever was on the radio.

The kids fell asleep on the sofa during *Free Willy*—which Janie insisted we watch—before poor Willy even jumped to freedom. For some reason, the whale's sagging dorsal fin made me incredibly sad every time I saw it.

Doc and I propelled them off to bed, skipping the whole teeth brushing ritual in spite of the M&M's and Milk Duds that they had along with their microwave popcorn. It was straight to bed, do not pass Go, no $200, just a pillow and a blanket and a mumbled "'night."

Mrs. B came out from cleaning up the kitchen, wiping her hands on a dish towel, just as Doc as I came back down the stairs. "Everyone tucked in?"

Doc pulled her against him, kissing her hard. "Everyone but us."

Mrs. B held her hand out for me and I melted in between them, snuggled up to her, Doc's crotch cradling the curve of my ass. Mrs. B's mouth was soft and warm, her tongue quickly finding mine. I could feel Doc's hands moving over her, around me, his cock lengthening against my bottom.

"I think we should go for a swim," she suggested into my ear, and I knew she was looking up at Doc. "One last midnight swim..."

It was only ten o'clock, but we all stood out on the beach in the moonlight, stripping naked on the sand. It was still warm, the day's heat dissipating slowly, but the water felt cool as I waded in after them. Mrs. B was already swimming out, but Doc lingered a little behind, waiting for me.

I dove under, getting my hair wet and slicking it back as I came up beside him. He looked down at me, reached for me, and I wrapped myself around him as we kissed, squeezing my thighs at his hips, bouncing a little in his arms.

"Throw me," I whispered in his ear, nibbling on it.

He laughed. "Are you sure?"

I nodded, grinning, as he grabbed my hips in his big hands, bending his knees a little before propelling me upward, squealing, into the air, just like he did to Henry and Janie. I came crashing down into the waves, holding my nose and sinking nearly to the bottom.

"Woo hoo!" I broke the surface. He was still laughing as Mrs. B swam back towards us, smiling. "Again!"

He did it again, and a third time, both he and Mrs. B laughing when I surfaced with a "woo-hoo!" The next time he grabbed my hips, though, he pulled me in close, and I could feel his erection nudging between my legs.

"Wanna go for a ride, little girl?" he asked into my ear and I could feel his fingers probing between my legs, searching out the slippery wetness there, parting my lips.

"My mommy told me not to go for rides with strangers," I teased, sighing deeply when his fingers found me, slipping into me.

"Do I look strange?" He played along, kissing me, a brief tonguing that slid down my chin and neck quickly to my breasts. As he sucked them, I heard him give a low growl, and felt Mrs. B's hand under the water beneath me, tugging on his cock. She was guiding him, me, in a slow, watery dance.

"Mommy says it's ok," she murmured into my ear, nudging his fingers out of the way with the tip of his cock, and I felt the swollen head seeking entrance. "Just this once..."

Groaning, I sank my flesh down over his shaft, wrapping my legs around his waist and digging my heels into his back. The water bobbed us all up and down, a natural rhythm, his cock slipping through me again and again. Mrs. B stood next to us, tugging at my nipples, leaning in to lick them.

"Ooooo yes!" I arched my back for her tongue as it made circles around my pink, pursed buds. She held me in the water as I floated on my back now, kissing me as Doc grabbed my hips and worked his cock into my pussy, pushing against the surf. We rode it, slow gentle waves coming in one after the other, a rise and fall that I could feel spreading through my belly.

I wrapped my arms around Mrs. B's neck, my tongue sucking hers in, moaning into her mouth as she tweaked my nipples and slid her hand down between my legs. Her fingers slipped over my mound, feeling where Doc was rocking his stiff flesh into my softness, and then climbed back up to my clit, staying there.

The waves seemed to swell and crest higher and higher, my cries lost in the sound of the surf. I was going to come and I clung to her, to him, both of them sending me over the edge into ecstasy. My pussy fluttered and then clamped down on Doc's shaft as I came, sucking him deep inside of me as I twisted in his hands, her arms.

"Yes, yes, yes," Mrs. B murmured, her fingers getting another shiver, two, three, out of me. "That's a good little girl."

Doc slowed, stopped, but didn't pull out of me. He was still hard, a pulsing heat inside of me as we floated together. I panted, breathless, into Mrs. B's neck and we just rocked in the moonlight, drifting.

"Let's go in." Mrs. B helped me sit, still impaled on Doc. He groaned, gripping my hips for a moment, holding me still.

We didn't say anything, we just gathered our clothes and went upstairs. Mrs. B started the shower, and we soaped each other, kissing, caressing, touching as we went. Her hand found its way between my legs again, slippery with soap, when I was kissing Doc, my fingers sliding wetly over his balls, cupping them, rolling.

"I should shave you again." She petted me there.

"I'll hold her," Doc offered and I gasped when he leaned against the tile, turning my back to him and hefting me in his arms.

"Doc!" I squealed as he grabbed my knees, bent them back, exposing me to Mrs. B. I could feel the hard muscles of his chest and belly working as he took my weight, holding me up for her.

"Perfect." Mrs. B chuckled, reaching for a razor she kept hanging on the shower organizer. She soaped me up good, rubbing hard to make a lather, and I gasped, twisting a little against Doc.

"Gotta hold still." She raked the razor upward from bottom to top. Mrs. B spread my lips with her fingers at the top, the razor riding the pink edge toward them.

"Am I too heavy?" I turned my head to look at Doc, seeing his eyes following the path of the razor between my legs. He just shook his head, pulling my knees back even further, rolling my hips up a little so he could see even more. Mrs. B's fingers slid over my mound, feeling for stray hairs. She teased my clit for a moment, making me sigh and moan.

When she reached for the showerhead, I grabbed her hand. "Wait."

Puzzled, she turned back to me as I slid her fingers down through my slit, past the little opening to my pussy, down further to my ass.

"Don't forget here," I murmured and she smiled, her eyes bright.

"Mmmmmm!" She slipped a finger into my ass, making me gasp and squirm. "Let's get your little asshole nice and clean, hm?" Doc groaned and I felt him shift, straining to see her finger probing between my cheeks, but he couldn't from that angle.

"Do you like that?" she breathed, her eyes on my face. Her finger was twisting, pushing a little deeper, slippery with soap and sliding easily in and out.

"Yes." I closed my eyes and leaned my head back on Doc's shoulder. He turned to kiss me, sucking my tongue into his mouth as Mrs. B continued working her finger deeper and deeper into my ass.

"Feels good doesn't it?" Doc nuzzled my cheek.

I met his eyes. "Will you put your cock there?"

He let out a breath. "Are you sure?"

"Yes." I nodded, finding his mouth again.

I didn't know if it was the margaritas, or the heat of the shower, or the feel of her finger probing the sensitive flesh of my asshole, or perhaps the thought of Gretchen telling me how much she loved it... maybe it was just that this was our last night here, and I wanted to give them something special.

I whispered it against his mouth, "I want you to fuck my ass."

The kiss broke as he lowered me slowly to my feet. My legs were tingly and a little numb and I clung to Mrs. B as she used the shower massage to rinse me off. We towel dried quickly and found our way into their bed, tumbling together, me between the two of them.

I kissed Mrs. B down to the bed, like she had me last night, spreading her thighs with mine, cupping her breasts in my hands. My baby-soft, smooth pussy rubbed up against hers and I shifted my hips from side to side, using my lips to spread hers lips, mashing our flesh together as we kissed.

Glancing over at Doc, seeing his cock in his hand, I groaned, resting my head against the soft pillow of Mrs. B's breasts.

"Are you sure?" Mrs. B stroked my hair.

I nodded, seeing the fire in Doc's eyes. "Yes. Come on, Doc."

He leaned over and opened the night table drawer, pulling out the white tube he'd used with Mrs. B and opening the cap. Mrs. B's fingers found my nipples, rolling, tugging, twisting, making me gasp as I watched him spread a generous amount of clear fluid over his cock.

Then he came to kneel between my thighs, his slick fingers gripping my ass, steadying me. I gasped when I felt him squirt something cold right against the tight, puckered hole of my ass. Mrs. B kissed my cheek, still thumbing my nipples, strumming them, making my pussy hum.

"Just my fingers," Doc murmured, probing.

My eyes flew open wide and Mrs. B cooed into my ear. "Shhh, it's ok."

His finger was much larger and thicker than hers as it slid slowly in. I gritted my teeth, closing my eyes, feeling the stretch and a little burn as he put another one in.

"Oh God!" I groaned, burying my face against Mrs. B's neck.

"You're so tense." She nuzzled me. "Relax...feel his fingers spreading you open..."

I was feeling it, and they seemed impossibly huge. I couldn't imagine how big his cock was going to feel and I was dreading it. Mrs. B's hands slid down over my ribcage, stroking the sides of my hips.

"Relax," she whispered. "Open up your bottom..."

I sighed, drew a shaky breath, and tried. His fingers were working slowly in and out, around and around, twisting inside that tight band of flesh, spreading me open.

"Good, Ronnie," Doc murmured and I felt him go deeper. "That's it... let me in."

Mrs. B slid her hand between my legs, cupping my mound. I sighed as her fingers started rubbing, making easy circles against my clit. It was a nice distraction from Doc's tight stretch into my ass.

"Are you ready?" Doc slid his fingers out.

I groaned, bracing myself, clenching my eyes closed tight. "Okay."

"No, sweetie." Mrs. B lifted my chin and made me look at her. The fingers between my legs didn't stop, stroking and petting my little clit, making me shiver.

"You have to be open." She traced my lips with her finger, kissing me. "Look into my eyes... stay right here with me... okay?"

I nodded, gasping when Doc shifted his weight, and I felt something huge—*enormous!*—pressing against my asshole. I clenched it, without thinking, biting my lip, feeling the fluted skin there squeezing around the very tip of his cock.

"It's okay." Mrs. B rubbed my clit a little faster now. I shook my head, but my eyes never left hers. "This is the hardest part, remember?"

"I'll go slow." Doc's hands were petting my ass, then opening it, spreading it for the head of his cock. I squirmed, feeling the push forward, the stretch of my flesh, that hot, crinkled hole resisting him. He petted me some more, murmuring, "Easy, easy..."

"Oh God—wait!" I moaned, feeling him give a little shove against that tender cleft, pushing into the taut band of muscle that wanted him out, out! "Please, God, wait!"

"Look at me," Mrs. B whispered. My jaw was clenched, my hands fists against the comforter on either side of her. Her eyes searched mine, and she said, "You want to push him out?"

I nodded, gasping. "Yes!"

"Then do it," she said. I gave her a puzzled look, frowning.

"Go ahead. Push," she urged, and I groaned, straining a little at the force seeking entrance to that tiny passageway.

Doc gasped, his hips moving forward, and I felt him slip further inside, the heat and swell of him incredible.

"Do it again." Mrs. B fingered my clit, my pussy trembling under her hand. "Push him out."

I groaned, using my muscles there to try to expel him, but the moment he shifted forward, I felt him slide into me. There was a little "pop" as his cock head slid under that ring of muscle that wanted to resist him.

I strained, gasping, realizing that the more I pushed, the deeper he could get. We struggled that way for a moment, Doc leaning into me, me pushing back at him, until I felt him pull me hard into the saddle of his hips, making me gasp.

"Good girl," Mrs. B murmured as I panted against her neck.

"Is there more?" I groaned, looking back at him.

He shook his head. "You've got it all, sweetie."

"Now comes the fun part." She kissed my sweaty neck. "Remember?"

Doc began to move inside of me, pulling out and pressing in. Mrs. B worked her fingers over my clit as my ass relaxed a little, feeling the thrust and shift of him as he began to fuck me. It was a slow ride at first, and I began to let go, my hands unclenching, my belly and thighs still quivering with their effort

"That's it." She used her other hand to cup my breast, her palm rubbing over my nipple. "Let him fuck you. Let him take you.

Her fingers were focused now, circling the hood of my clit through all the wetness, thumbing my nipple, making me rock and moan with pleasure. The cock in my ass moved easily now, that tight band of muscle still pulling and pushing with every thrust, but I wasn't doing it anymore. I was just letting it go.

"Does that feel good?" Mrs. B asked. "Do you like that big cock filling your little asshole?"

I groaned, not answering, still not sure. It was so big, and I felt *so full...*

"Do you want me to lick your little pussy while he fucks your ass?" She tugged on my clit, grazing it with her fingernail.

"Oh God!" I moaned, looking at her. "Yes... yes..."

She smiled, shifting out from underneath me. "Turn her over, Doc."

"No!" I panicked. I knew I couldn't take him into me again, I just couldn't, but he was turning me, rolling me to my back, his cock going balls deep as he brought my legs up, making me gasp at the sensation. Mrs. B was over by the dresser, and I saw with wide eyes that she had her black vibrator in her hand.

"See?" Mrs. B climbed on top of me, her pussy over my face as she leaned in to lick my clit. "Not so bad..."

Mrs. B was soaking wet, her lips thick and fat and swollen as I parted them with my tongue. She rocked her hips, groaning, her fingers slipping into me as her mouth covered my mound. Her tongue was soft and lapping at me as Doc pressed my legs back further, his cock never stopping, shoving into me deeper now, so deep I wondered where he was inside of me, the tip of his cock lost in my belly somewhere.

"Ohhhhhh, Mrs. B!" I cried when she twisted and turned that big, hard cock at the entrance of my pussy, slipping the head in. It was tight, Doc's shaft already filling my ass, but she pressed on, sliding the black length into my pink heat—and then turning it on.

"Oh God!" I groaned, being fucking by two cocks now, one in my pussy, the other in my ass, both of them moving in unison, stretching me wide.

"Now that's filled," Mrs. B murmured before she found my clit again with her tongue.

"Jesus." Doc's grip tighten on my ankles, shoving my legs back as Mrs. B fucked me with that humming black cock. I realized that he must feel it, too, that deep buzz in my pelvis. She fucked me, he fucked me, and I was lost, moaning, rocking, aching all over.

"Oh yes!" I growled, bucking. "Fuck me! Fuck my ass and my cunt!"

They both murmured something, some appreciation for my words, but I couldn't hear them. I was lost in the buzzing heat of being fucked, two cocks filling me again and again until I thought I might pass out from the pleasure of it.

The cock in my ass had a give and a softness, even though he was hard as a rock, that the cock in my pussy didn't have. It was unforgiving, relentless, a dark, black buzzing heat pressing deep into my pink hole.

"Please!" I begged, spreading, rocking, wanting more and more. "Oh I love that big cock in my ass and my cunt!"

"Good girl... lick my pussy, sweetie." Mrs. B wiggled her ass, rocking her pink, wet flesh against my tongue.

Dazed, I wrapped my arms around her hips, pulling her into my mouth, rubbing my whole face between her legs as I sucked on her clit. It went on and on, Mrs. B against my tongue, Doc fucking me harder and harder, grunting with the effort, the vibrator humming deep inside of me as she licked me until I was trembling.

"Oh baby!" Mrs. B moaned, spreading wider. "Don't stop! I'm gonna cum all over your face..."

I gasped, sucking her, swallowing, my tongue working her clit until I felt her shudder against me, her moans sending deep vibrations through my pelvis. Her juices flowed down over my chin and cheeks, covering her thighs, her pussy spasming again and again.

"Oh fuck!" Doc groaned, and I knew he was close, his cock was like steel in my ass as he pumped into my flesh. "Oh fuck, baby, I can't stop it."

"Come on!" Mrs. B was still shuddering with her own climax. "Come for me, Doc!"

He growled as Mrs. B eased him out of my ass. I moaned as she aimed him at my clit and I felt the first wave of his white heat spurting there, the vibrator still humming deep inside my pussy. He grunted and thrust into her hand, his cum making fiery, hot trails down my slit and around that humming black cock.

Mrs. B began to lick it all up, still working the vibrator into me, fucking me as she sucked his cum off my clit. I couldn't stand it, and I bucked beneath her, my pussy clenching that black cock tight as I came in her mouth. She was moaning and licking at me, making wet, sucking noises between my legs.

"Oh God, oh God, Mrs. B!" I groaned as she eased the cock out of my pussy. I was still shuddering as she turned it off and rolled onto her back on the bed. She brought the vibrator up to me, putting the head against my lips. I accepted it, sucking it into my mouth as Doc groaned and settled on the other side of me.

Doc took it in his hand, too, watching it disappear between my lips as my eyes flicked between them. They were both wearing soft, bemused smiles as they watched me lick and swallow my own juices.

"Again?" I looked between them and they smiled, their eyes meeting over my head.

"As much as you want." Mrs. B set the vibrator aside and kissed my mouth.

Doc groaned. "Just let me recharge my batteries first."

I glanced down at the vibrator on the bed. "Hey... that one doesn't need recharging."

Mrs. B laughed, glancing at Doc. "I think we created a monster."

I snuggled down between them, giggling, so full I felt I could simply burst.

Chapter Fifteen

I was dreaming about the dolphins, playing in the waves, riding their backs like silver bullets through the water. Their bodies were sleek and soft between my thighs and I rocked as we rode, feeling that familiar tingle. I woke up flushed, gasping, remembering the power surfing between my legs. Mrs. B's thigh was nestled between mine, her breath warm and sweet over my face. Doc's arm was draped over her hip.

Watching them sleep in the dimness, I felt my belly clench. We were going home today. Home felt like a dream. This, here, in bed together, felt real. I slipped slowly out from under Mrs. B's arm, untangling myself and grabbing my clothes, pulling them quickly on. I glanced at the clock and saw that it wasn't even six yet. I opened their door, peeking into the hallway. Janie and Henry's doors were closed.

Going back to my bed felt too empty, and instead I went downstairs and out to the beach. It was humid, not hot yet, though. There was a slight breeze, actually enough to give me goose bumps as I spread out a blanket. The rhythmic sound of the waves was like a slow heartbeat as the sky started to lighten along the horizon.

I heard the door wall open behind me and looked up to see Mrs. B slipping out, shutting it behind her. She smiled as she came to lie next to me wearing a white pair of shorts and a black tank top. I returned her smile and we didn't say anything for a while, we just listened to the waves and watched the sky grow lighter by degrees.

"Home today," I reminded us both with a sigh, rolling onto my elbow to look at her.

"Yes." She reached her hand out and tugged at the side of my shorts. "But you got nice and brown this week, didn't you?"

"Yeah." I pulled them aside, showing her the white string-line from the bikini that ran along the bend of my thigh.

When I lifted my eyes, I saw hers focused there and smiled. "But that's not all I got..." I pulled my shorts aside even more, showing her my shaved mound.

"Mmmm, no," Mrs. B breathed, moving her hand to cover my pussy, petting it with her fingertips. "Not all..."

I closed my eyes at her touch, craving it, aching for more. I wanted to commit everything about this moment to memory—the feel of her fingernails tickling the inside of my thigh, the smell of her hair as she leaned over to kiss me, the sound of the water swelling and receding.

Breathing her in as her lips found mine, I pulled her down to me, hungry. She moaned at my response, my hands lifting her shirt, pulling it off her in a hurry, wanting to feel her full, lush body pressed to mine. I tugged my own shirt off, wiggling out of my shorts, devouring her mouth with mine as we rolled on the blanket.

I found myself on top of her as we kissed, her hands all over me, everywhere at once. I smiled as I licked and sucked at her throat, remembering how shy I had been not too long ago in her arms. Now I was eager, sucking and licking at the heavy globes of her breasts, making my way to their big, brown centers.

Mrs. B gave a deep sigh, sliding her hand down between her thighs, under the elastic band, and I felt her movements between my own legs. It sent sweet jolts of pleasure through my pussy to be bare against the fabric of her shorts while she rubbed herself underneath them, her nipples hardening against my tongue.

I wanted her pussy against mine, and I knelt between her thighs, yanking her shorts down over her hips. She gave me a dreamy smile, and I could see her fingers now, moving between her lips, rubbing back and forth over her clit. I wanted to taste her, but I wanted to feel her more. I slithered my body across hers, straddling her at an angle, so our legs made that delicious X-shape that would get our pussies as close together as possible.

"Mmmmm, God I love that." Her fingers stayed between us, spreading us both open. She put her knees up, rocking with me as I smeared my juices over hers, the wet sound of us together competing with the pounding of the surf. Closing my eyes, I ground my hips in circles, feeling the folds of her flesh, all soft, tender pinkness, rubbing against mine.

I tried to make our clits kiss, lost in the slippery darkness of sensation, pressing my pussy faster and faster toward release. Her breath was coming more quickly and I looked down to see her pulling and tugging at her nipples. As I watched, she lifted one of her breasts towards her mouth and licked at the fat bud in the center. Her lips closed around it and sucked, pulling the whole thing into her mouth.

I cupped my own breasts, lifting them, trying, knowing my tongue wouldn't reach. Instead, I pinched my nipples, rolling them, sending additional little shocks of pleasure down to my pelvis, where my clit was nudging hers. She was rolling like thunder under me now, moaning and meeting me with every pass.

"Are you close?" I slid my hand down, feeling the wet squelch of us together, the slickness of her lips.

"Yes, oh, God, yes!" She moaned, and I knew I wouldn't quite make it with her, but I wanted to send her over. I slipped my hand past the entrance of her pussy, finding the tender, puckered hole of her ass. She gasped and bucked as I probed, pressing my finger into that sensitive flesh.

"Oooooo!" She howled with it, and I felt her orgasm in the muscles of her ass, trying to rhythmically push my finger back out as she twisted and rocked. I could feel myself near the edge but wanted to hang onto it, to keep feeling this high. She had never looked so beautiful as she did in that moment with my finger pressed into her ass and my pussy splayed across hers, making her come so hard she was quivering all over with it.

I wanted her, and I took her while she was still shuddering with her climax, turning and burying my face into her wet, pink flesh. She gasped and moaned and shook underneath me, but she accepted my tongue lapping and poking through her hot folds. I wiggled my pussy over her face and rocked when her mouth found my clit, sucking and tonguing me like she was going to devour my flesh.

It wasn't long before she took me there—I was already dangling at that edge, my pussy pulsing with a full, throbbing ache. She just used her tongue centered right over my clit, a fast, steady rhythm that sent me over the edge without a chance to look back.

"Ohhhh God!" I felt that hot, delicious burst of pleasure rocking my body, pressing my pussy against her face, drowning her in my juices.

"Mmmmmm!" She still lapped at me, slow, her fingernails grazing over my swollen lips. "Let's do that again."

I groaned, locking my mouth back down over her slit, digging in deep with my tongue, greedy to taste more of her. She didn't stop licking me, her fingers spreading me open, sliding inside of me, pumping in and out. It made me long for a cock to pound me as she tongued her way through my flesh.

She spread her legs wide, pulling them back, giving me more of her, and I took it, probing my fingers deep into her pussy, twisting and massaging inside, pressing her open. I could see her asshole winking at me, and I pressed there, too, with my other hand, using my index finger to probe that furrowed flesh.

Neither of us could talk, our mouths busy, our tongues lapping, but our muffled cries and moans were like two hungry kittens kneading their mother's belly for milk, wanting more, more. Mrs. B's finger found its way to my ass, too, and I gasped and gulped more of her as I rocked against her hand, driving her deeper.

I could feel how close she was, how close I was, and I couldn't hold it back, as much as I wanted it to go on forever. The exquisite torture had to end, and it did, exploding between us like a dam breaking, our bodies tumbling and rolling together as we gasped and moaned and trembled with it.

Turning, finding her mouth again, we kissed, our faces full of each other, my lips sliding across her wet cheeks. We giggled together, hugging, rocking, and I realized that the sun was really coming up, now, the sky glowing orange across the horizon, and her hair reflected it, glowing golden in the morning light.

"Let's go wake up Doc," I whispered against her neck, licking there, my mouth still wet with her.

Mrs. B chuckled, squeezing me. "Come on."

We pulled our clothes on, just in case we met Janie or Henry in the hallway, but the house was still quiet. I eased their door open, finding Doc snoring on his back, the covers thrown off, his cock pointing toward the ceiling.

"Wonder what he's dreaming about." I grinned as Mrs. B shut the door behind us. She smiled, stripping off her clothes and I did, too. We eased up onto the bed, each of us stalking up a side, both reaching for his cock with our tongues. I don't know when he actually woke up—I was too lost in the slick feel of Mrs. B's mouth against mine over the spongy head of his cock—but I did hear him murmuring, and then moaning, and finally, I felt his hand in my hair.

When I looked up at him, he was watching us with half-closed eyes. "I was dreaming about something like this."

"Thought you might be." I flicked down his shaft with my tongue, my fingers grazing his balls. "You were hard as a rock."

"Couldn't let that go to waste, baby." Mrs. B sucked the head, her mouth making sloppy wet noises.

"I'm a lucky man." He groaned as I slithered up against him, wrapping my thighs around his as I kissed his lips. Mrs. B continued to work her mouth over his cock, making soft, happy noises in her throat.

Doc smiled at me, his hand cupping my ass, pulling me in tight. "You taste familiar."

"I should." I grinned, squeezing my thighs around his. "I just had your wife for breakfast."

"Still hungry?" His eyes closed for a moment as Mrs. B took him all the way into her mouth.

"Always." I slipped my leg over his belly, moving onto him in a straddle.

He held my hips in his hands, his eyes moving over my body. "Beautiful."

I just smiled, wiggling down, closer and closer to his cock. I looked over my shoulder at Mrs. B and saw that she was stroking him, aiming him. Leaning forward, splaying my hands on his chest, I gave her access to my pussy, still wet from her mouth.

"I wanna ride," I whispered, looking back at Doc. He nodded, groaning as Mrs. B slipped the swollen head of his cock through my waiting lips. I felt the tip nudge my hole and sank down onto his length, taking all of him inside of me.

Closing my eyes, I waited, savoring that first exquisite moment, feeling Mrs. B's hands moving over my hips, down between Doc's thighs, caressing his balls. When I opened them again, Doc was looking between my legs where he had completely disappeared into my flesh. His fingers probed there, spreading me, brushing my clit and making me squirm.

"Beautiful little cunt." He squeezed my clit between his thumb and forefinger.

I started grinding, just moving my hips around in circles, rubbing the head of his cock deep inside me. He let out a breath, a little groan, rubbing my clit with his thumb as I danced on his shaft, letting it touch every soft part inside of me. Mrs. B crawled up next to Doc, laying beside him, kissing his mouth, using her palms to rub over his hard, broad chest, flicking his nipples.

It was a slow ride, and I started using my legs, sliding up on his shaft and then down again, grinding into him for a moment before doing it again. My clit was humming underneath his thumb, and I watched Mrs. B spreading her pussy open, rubbing herself as she watched us.

"Look at that," Mrs. B whispered into Doc's ear as he grabbed my hips, rocking me a little faster. "Do you like that little nineteen-year-old cunt?"

"Fuck!" He moaned, moving me back and forth over his cock. "She's so tight, baby."

Mrs. B made an "mmmmm" sound, her eyes between our legs, her fingers moving faster. I moaned as I rubbed my own clit, closing my eyes, lost in the trembling pleasure of it. Doc was fucking up against me, his cock swelling between my legs. I squeezed his shaft with my pussy, making him moan.

I gasped when he rolled me over onto my back, shoving my thighs with his, pressing them back, hooking my feet against his shoulders. He was driving into me, now, his mouth searching out mine, sucking my tongue deep into his mouth. I moaned and raked my nails over his shoulders, down his arms, his cock sliding along a slick path over my clit again and again as he fucked me.

"That's it, baby." Mrs. B was next to us on her side, one knee pulled back, her fingers fucking herself as she watched. "Fuck that sweet little cunt. Fuck her hard."

"Yesssss!" I moaned, meeting her eyes, then his. "Please!"

"Please what?" Doc used his weight to drive into me hard, holding himself there, straining.

I moaned, wiggling my hips, wanting him. "Fuck me!" He gave me a little more, his shaft teasing my clit. "Oh yeah, come on, Doc. Fuck my hot, wet cunt!"

He groaned, thrusting into me again, his hips working against mine. I looked up into his eyes and could see he was waiting for me, trying to hold back.

"Do you like my wet little puss?" I rocked my pelvis into his, meeting his thrusts with my own. "My tight... little... cunt?" I punctuated each word with a squeeze of my muscles around his shaft.

"Oh fuck!" He gasped, biting his lip, slowing. I squeezed him again, long and hard, feeling the throb and swell of him inside of me.

"Little minx!" He pulled his shaft all the way back, and I looked down to see it poised at the entrance of my pussy, slick and pulsing.

"Don't you like it?" I teased, squeezing my muscles again, this time just around the tip, trying to draw him back in. "So wet and hot and tight?"

"Brat." He grabbed his cock, kneeling up between my legs, slapping my pussy with it.

"Ohh!" I gasped, feeling the head rubbing against my clit. He rocked like that, moving the tip back and forth in my wetness. I moaned, looking over at Mrs. B. Her fingers were moving deep into her pussy, her eyes between our legs.

"Like that?" He reached up and squeezed my nipples, working the head of his cock through my slit.

"Oh, Doc!" I moaned, wrapping my legs around him. "Oh God!"

"More?" He rubbed it faster, pressing the tip harder.

I squirmed, flushing, gasping, so close I couldn't stand it. He slid a finger into my mouth and I sucked on it, an instinctive thing, and just that sent me over, moaning and sucking and rocking as my orgasm shook me like a little earthquake. He smiled, still rubbing the head against my sensitive clit, making me shudder.

"Now, you little cock tease…" He grinned, leaning in and kissing me hard, making me flush. "Get up onto my cock and really ride me."

I groaned as he went to his back, his slick cock pointing skyward, waiting for me. Trembling, I climbed onto him, reaching between my legs for his shaft, but he grabbed my hips, guiding me, sinking his cock up into me in one swift motion.

"Carrie…" Doc held his hand out to her as I started to rock, still shivering from my orgasm. "Come here, baby."

She smiled, coming to him, letting him move her leg over his head. Facing me, she settled over his mouth and I could see how wet her lips were, glistening as he probed his tongue there.

"Come here." She wrapped her arms around me, kissing me deeply.

I moaned into her mouth, feeling the soft pressure of her full breasts against mine, her nipples grazing my flesh. We kissed and moaned and rocked that way. I could hear Doc moaning between her thighs and I couldn't resist squeezing his cock with my pussy. He pressed up hard into me, rolling his hips, making me gasp against Mrs. B's neck.

"Oh Doc!" She moaned, her nails digging into my back, her breasts pressed flat against my chest. "Oh baby, honey, God… yes!"

I felt her climax starting, a little tremor, a gasp, her teeth grazing my shoulder, and then it overtook her. I put my arms around her, holding her when she let herself collapse against me, moaning and shaking as she came. Doc was lapping at her still, making soft noises in his throat, and I could feel his cock swelling even bigger inside of me.

"Beautiful." Doc slapped her ass, making her squeal. "Now, you'd better get down there to catch all my cum in that sweet little mouth of yours."

Mrs. B smiled at me, her eyes still dazed. "Wanna share?"

I climbed off his cock, moving between his legs with Mrs. B as my hand moved up and down the wet shaft. He was watching us, his breath coming faster as I stroked him. Mrs. B put her mouth over the head, rolling her tongue around, making him gasp.

"Faster!" He moaned, and I tugged harder, working the skin over the head, squeezing as I came up on the shaft, pumping it into her mouth. "Ahhhhh fuck, get ready, baby!"

Mrs. B stuck her tongue out for it and I aimed the red, wet tip right there. Doc growled, his hips bucking again and again as his cock began to spew hot, white cum into her mouth. She rounded her tongue and I watched, my breath caught, as he flooded it with the thick fluid like it was a little cup made just for that purpose.

Her eyes were on mine, watching me pump his cock in my fist, but I couldn't stop staring at his cum welling up over the curve of her tongue. I leaned it and slid my tongue between her lips, tasting him, and she moaned and pressed her tongue to mine, his cum flowing between us and we were both swallowing the heat of him as we kissed.

"God!" Doc's hand moved in my hair. "Good girls." Mrs. B went to snuggle up with Doc, but I glanced at the clock, still shivering with the taste of him in my throat.

"I should go to my room," I murmured. "Have to pack..."

Mrs. B sighed and Doc grabbed my wrist as I went to climb off the bed.

"Hey," he said. "You ok?"

I smiled back at him, a slow heat flooding my chest.

"Yes." I nodded, knowing for the first time that I was telling him the truth. I was just fine

* * * *

It was so crazy over Christmas, and then with the start of my new term, that I didn't even think about the Baumgartners not calling me. Well, that wasn't entirely true, but at least I was too busy to think about it much. I didn't want to admit, even to myself, how much I missed them.

It wasn't until I saw Gretchen in the mall that I was really overwhelmed with the memory of it, making me flushed and warm just seeing her standing in the food court, tucking her long blonde hair behind her ear and laughing.

I was watching her so closely, flooded in memory, that I didn't even see who was sitting with her at first.

"Ronnie!" Janie waved, her eyes bright.

I threaded my way through the tables toward them. Gretchen had seen me and she was smiling, holding her hand out to me. She hugged me when I reached them and I had to fight not to gasp out loud when I felt her body pressed to mine.

"God, I've missed you," she murmured as the kids jumped up, Janie hugging me around the waist, Henry tugging at my ponytail. "I meant to call, but it's been so crazy..."

"Me, too." I smiled at the kids. "How was your Christmas, you guys?"

They both started talking at once, giving me a litany of things they'd opened Christmas morning. My eyes never left Gretchen's face, that warm look spreading through me to my toes.

"I'm working for them, now," Gretchen explained over their heads. "I'm the Baumgartner's au pair."

I raised my eyebrows, letting the kids pull me into a seat as they continued to vie for my attention.

"Do you want to do something tonight?" Gretchen asked, and I looked at the hem of her skirt riding up her thigh as she crossed one knee over the other. "Just you and me."

I realized I wouldn't be babysitting for the Baumgartners anymore, but watching Gretchen's eyes on me, her smile so warm it was like heat, I knew it didn't matter

"Yeah." I nodded, smiling back at her. "Let's do... something."

I felt her knee against mine under the table and shivered, realizing that I felt truly happy for the first time since we'd come home.

The End

ABOUT SELENA KITT

Like any feline, Selena Kitt loves the things that make her purr—and wants nothing more than to make others purr right along with her! Pleasure is her middle name, whether it's a short cat nap stretched out in the sun or a long kitty bath. She makes it a priority to explore all the delightful distractions she can find, and follow her vivid and often racy imagination wherever it wants to lead her.

Her writing embodies everything from the spicy to the scandalous, but watch out—this kitty also has sharp claws and her stories often include intriguing edges and twists that take readers to new, thought-provoking depths.

When she's not pawing away at her keyboard, Selena runs an innovative publishing company (www.excessica.com) and in her spare time, she worships her devoted husband, corrals four kids and a dozen chickens, all while growing an organic garden. She also loves bellydancing and photography.

Her e-publishing credits include: *Rosie's Promise* published by Samhain and *Torrid Teasers #49* published by <u>Whiskey Creek Press</u> featuring two short stories, *French Lessons* and *I'll Be Your Superman* in 2008. Her stories and poems are in the following anthologies: <u>*Coming Together: For The Cure*</u>, <u>*Coming Together: Under Fire*</u> and <u>*Coming Together Volume 1*</u> and <u>*Volume 3*</u>. Two stories, <u>*Sacred Spots*</u> and <u>*Happy Accident*</u>, have been published by <u>Phaze Publishing</u>, and her novels *Christmas Stalking*, *Blind Date*, *The Surrender of Persephone* and *The Song of Orpheus* are coming soon. She has also been published online in <u>The Shadow Sacrament: a journal of sex and spirituality</u>, <u>The Erotic Woman</u>, and her story, *Connections*, was one of the runners-up for the <u>2006 Rauxa Prize</u>, given annually to an erotic short story of "exceptional literary quality," out of over 1,000 nominees, where awards are judged by a select jury and all entries are read "blind" (without author's name available.) She can be reached on her website at <u>www.selenakitt.com</u>

If you liked
<u>Babysitting the Baumgartners</u>, try:

BLUEBEARD'S WIFE

Tara's husband has never shared a fantasy with her, or even masturbated—that she knows of. However, this curious wife discovers a phone bill full of phone calls to sex lines and realizes her husband has been living a double life! Instead of getting mad, Tara's curiosity leads her to begin listening in on John's steamy conversations in hopes of finding out what he really wants in the bedroom. After several failed attempts at bringing fantasy to reality, however, a frustrated Tara turns to her much more adventurous best friend, Kelly, for help. A quick psychology 101 diagnosis from Dr. Kelly marks John as having a classic "madonna/whore" complex, and she quickly sets about making plans to rectify this situation. Tara goes along for the ride, hoping that Kelly may have the answer to bridging the seemingly ever-growing gap in her marriage...

Warning: This title contains a MFF threesome, a daddy/daughter role play between consenting adults, strong language, minor drug use and lesbian and anal sex.

What People are Saying
about Bluebeard's Wife:

<u>Mmmm....excellent storytelling!</u>
Holy Mackerel! You are SO good at this. There's something highly erotic about a married couple pushing their sexual envelope and you have captured it perfectly.

<u>Beautifully Nuanced</u>
Just gorgeous—incredibly erotic, but also a beautiful exploration of a woman's sexuality. Keep up the great work.

EXCERPT from <u>BLUEBEARD'S WIFE</u>:

We ended up closing the place down, John and I. Kelly and Chris headed home about midnight, and I sat and finished another bottle of wine while I watched John move among the tables, talking and laughing. He helped me on with my coat when it was time to go, and held my elbow as we walked to the car.

"Are you drunk?" he asked me as he got into driver's side.

I looked over at him in the dimness. "Are you mad?

"Am I mad that you're drunk? Or am I mad that you were out dirty dancing with your girlfriend at my company Christmas party?" John started the car and put it in reverse.

"Um… that, or… whatever," I said, struggling with my seat belt. I couldn't seem to find the slot to put it into. John accelerated hard and I was propelled back against the seat. I was still trying to get my seat belt fastened when John hit the brakes at a stop sign and I jolted forward, reaching out my hand to the dashboard to catch myself, but my reflexes were slow, and I missed.

"What were you thinking?" John asked with a sigh, reaching over and doing my seat belt up for me.

I felt tears sting my eyes and looked out the passenger window so he wouldn't see them. "I don't know," I whispered. "I guess maybe that you might think I was sexy."

We didn't talk again until John backed the car into the garage. He always backed in, so he could pull put in a hurry in the morning. Then he turned to me in the dark of the car, his voice low. "Tara, do you know what I wanted to do to you when you came downstairs in that dress?"

I shook my head, turning a little toward him.

John reached a hand out and fingered the soft, satin hem that was riding high on my thighs. "I wanted to tear it off you."

"You did?" I asked, my eyes wide. He was looking down at where my dress ended.

"I wanted to tear it off you and take you, right there, up against the wall in the hallway." His voice was hoarse, and I swallowed hard.

"You did?" I squeaked.

"Seeing you dancing out there with Kelly—you don't know how sexy you are, do you?" he asked, leaning over to me, his hand running up from my knee to my thigh. His breath was warm on my face, and I could smell the 7&7's he'd been drinking all night. My own head was still swimming with wine.

"You two rubbing up against each other, seeing your red little dress riding up and up," he whispered, his hand pushing my dress up further as he sought higher ground on my leg. "You looked just like you do when you come, with your eyes half closed and your mouth open and your legs quivering."

I moaned, tilting my face up to him, and then he was kissing me, his tongue forcing its way past my teeth, down my throat, as he pressed me into the door. "I wanted to fuck you right there on the dance floor," he growled against my neck, biting and sucking at my flesh. "I wanted to fuck you both."

I gasped, his hands groping me in the dark, everywhere at once. My dress was pushed up to my waist now, his fingers rubbing fast and hard between my legs. We kissed, our mouths meshing together as he leaned over the gearshift to get to me. When he pulled my panties aside and plunged his fingers into me, I hissed, putting one foot up onto the dashboard to give him better access.

He was trying to climb over onto me but there wasn't enough room—not in his little Roadster. When I whispered that fact to him, he grunted, pulling his hand away from me and moving to open his door. A moment later, he was opening mine, and I was still sitting there with my panties askew, my heels off, and my dress shoved up to my waist, struggling with the seatbelt.

He leaned over me and popped the button, pulling me out of the car and crushing me to him, his tongue digging deep into my mouth. I clung to him, wrapping my arms around his neck, feeling his hands roaming over my ass, squeezing and lifting me, pressing my crotch to his. I could feel how hard he was through his trousers.

Then he was turning me around, pressing me over the hood of the car, shoving my dress up higher on my waist. His hands moved over my ass, my thighs, and I heard his zipper and the felt his cock pressing against my panties. He shoved those aside, his fingers finding me again, moving in and out of my wetness— and I was wet, soaking wet, my panties moist with my heat.

He didn't bother to take them off, he just replaced his fingers with his cock, shoving himself deep inside me with a growl. I moaned, pressing my cheek to the metal, the engine still ticking as he started to fuck me, my hands out in front of me, just letting him take me. I could see the Christmas lights of the neighbor's house across the street, a blurred red and green glow as he rocked me against the Beemer's electric blue hood. He hadn't even shut the garage door.

"You like that?" he whispered, grinding his pelvis into me, his cock buried so deep it almost hurt. I couldn't catch my breath to answer, I just whimpered, but I arched my back and pressed against him in response.

He reached over me, grabbing my arms and twisting them behind my back. I gasped, wriggling and moaning, as he held my wrists with one hand, still fucking me, harder now, driving me against the cold side panel of the car. He slapped my ass with the other hand, making me squirm. The hot sting felt good in the night air.

I could see my breath, panting out in white streams toward Mr. Klein's house across the way—and

I could see Mr. Klein, walking across his living room. I wondered if he might be able to see us, and the thought was beyond exciting.

John was grunting with every thrust, his breath ragged. My panties were snug between my legs and every time he shoved into me, he pulled them up tight between my lips and effectively massaged my clit, the friction building up as he fucked me, really rapidly now, all the way into me, working hard.

"Oh God," I cried, feeling his hand tighten around my wrists, pulling me back against him and driving deeper, deeper still, into my pussy. "John, make me come!"

I could still see Mr. Klein, and I think he was at his window, but I didn't care. I ground myself back against John's cock, wanting more and more, until I couldn't breathe, I couldn't think. I was dizzy with wanting, feeling the ache between my legs moving toward release.

John grabbed my hip with his other hand, forcing himself hard up into me, growling and grinding, "Ahhhh God, baby, take my cum!" Feeling the first wave of him, hot and pulsing, coupled with his hips pounding against mine, forced me over, too, and I came hard, my pussy squeezing him, milking him.

"Ohhh yes, ohhhh!" I moaned, thrashing on the hood of the car, quivering beneath him.

He pulled out of me, and the cold of the night rushed in, making me shiver. He didn't let go of my wrists, turning me around to kiss me, his mouth a little softer now, but not much, his tongue still probing deep, his bare thighs pressing me back against the car, my ass resting against the cool edge.

"Now," he whispered, keeping me pressed against him, his hand still tight around my wrists wrapped behind my back. "Do you believe me, that I think you're sexy?"

I smiled, feeling dizzy, wrapping my leg around him, digging my heel into the back of his thigh. "Yes," I breathed, kissing him and holding on tight…

BUY THIS AND MORE TITLES AT
www.eXcessica.com

eXcessica's <u>BLOG</u>

www.excessica.com/blog

eXcessica's <u>YAHOO GROUP</u>

groups.yahoo.com/group/eXcessica/

Check out both for updates about eXcessica books,

as well as chances to win free E-Books!

And look for these other titles from Selena Kitt:

NAUGHTY BITS
By Selena Kitt

David has been brightening up his gray Surrey, England days with the porn collection hidden in his parents' shed, but when he find that his older sister, Dawn has discovered his magazine collection, things really begin to heat up. Their parents insist that their just-graduated son look for a job, but their daughter has the week off and is determined to work on her tan. Distracted David finds himself increasingly tempted by his seductive older sister, who makes it very clear what she wants. Her teasing ways slowly break down the taboo barrier between brother and sister until they both give in to their lust... but what are they going to do about the feelings that have developed between them in the meantime...?

Warning: This title contains incest and anal sex.

<u>ESCAPING FATE</u>
By Selena Kitt

Sam has an unusual interest in humans—well, considering she's a fairy of fate whose profession it is to determine their futures, it's no wonder! But it isn't just Karma she's curious about... Sam has what her fairy-pal Alex thinks is an inordinate and rather wanton interest in certain biological aspects of human behavior—most notably, *s-e-x*.

When Sam's job leads her into the path of a handsome man who rocks her world, Sam's interest becomes obsession. Alex reminds her that fairies get one Christmas wish – will Sam consider using hers to become human to experience one night of bliss?

When things become even more complicated—Sam discovers that Drew, the sexy stranger she's been fantasizing about, can actually *see* her—Sam finds herself immersed in a complex and tangled web of human experience. She has to make a choice that will teach her a twisted lesson in fate, ultimately change the course of human existence and even reveal the origin of Santa Claus!

Warning: Contains graphic language and sex.

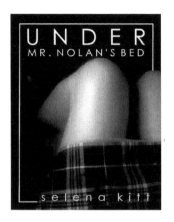

UNDER MR. NOLAN'S BED
By Selena Kitt

Leah and Erica have been best friends and have gone to the same Catholic school since just about forever. Leah spends so much time with the Nolans—just Erica and her handsome father, now, since Erica's mother died—that she's practically part of the family. When the girls find something naughty under Mr. Nolan's bed, their strict, repressive upbringing makes it all the more exciting as they begin their sexual experimentation. Leah's exploration presses deeper, and eventually she finds herself torn between her best friend and her best friend's father—but even she couldn't have predicted the shocking and bittersweet outcome of their affair.

Warning: This title contains a threesome, lesbian sex and incest.

THE SYBIAN CLUB
By Selena Kitt

Tasha convinces her husband, Max, to buy her a the ultimate female pleasure machine – a Sybian – but he only agrees if she can come up with a business plan to pay for it. Determined to keep her promise, she creates The Sybian Club and begins bringing women to the basement room set up just for her new toy. It becomes so popular, she has to enlist the help of new friend, Ashley, to keep up with the demand, and the women enjoy an exciting ride as the business thrives. But Tasha has developed feelings for Ashley, and doesn't know how to tell her husband that she wants to add more to their sex life than just a new toy...

Warning: This title contains a threesome, lesbian and anal sex.

STARVING ARTIST
By Selena Kitt

Ellie is living the life of a true starving artist in a small efficiency apartment in dangerous downtown Detroit, but more dangerous than her surroundings are the men to whom she pays rent. Denied help by her prosecutor father, who believes his daughter is wasting her life in art school, Ellie finds herself in a precarious position and surrenders helplessly to her predicament. However, a strange twist of fate gives Ellie a chance at revenge. Will she take it?

Warning: This title contains graphic language, nonconsensual and anal sex.

ON CHERRY HILL
By Selena Kitt

Midwife Anne gets pulled over in the middle of the night on Cherry Hill Road. She's on her way to a birth, but her urgency doesn't sway the unsympathetic officer. When the cop discovers something suspicious on Anne's driving record and insists she get out of the car, she knows she's in real trouble. When he cuffs her and bends her over the hood, things go beyond trouble...

But the surprising outcome of this tale gives both Anne and the reader a jolt they never could have anticipated...

Warning: This title contains graphic language and nonconsensual sex.

TICKLED PINK
By Selena Kitt

Who says sex can't be fun - or funny? You'll find more than enough amusing mishaps and uproarious situations to tickle your funny bone–and more!–in this delightfully wicked and delightfully sexy anthology from Selena Kitt.

Warning: This title contains graphic language and sex.

PAPERBACK ROMANCE
by Selena Kitt

Maya's heart yearns for romance and adventure, so that's what she writes about - but James Reardon, her college creative writing professor, insists she's wasting both time and talent. Determined to prove him wrong, Maya stumbles onto the fact that her professor's been keeping secrets - not the least of which is his attraction to her. Faced with a choice, she will have to decide whether or not to reveal his secret to the world–and her own desire for a man nearly twice her age.

Warning: This title contains graphic language and sex.

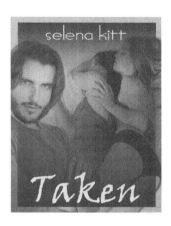

TAKEN
By Selena Kitt

Lizzy's friendship with her older boss, Sarah, turns into something deeper and much more exciting one rainy day after work, and Lizzy finds herself drawn into a world she never knew existed. Sarah has a dominant streak, and as she leads Lizzy into the role of a submissive, the two women become closer than they ever thought possible. But while Sarah, hurt too many times, wears a ring, and tells guys she's "taken," Lizzy knows she secretly longs for a man. Determined to find one for them both to share, Lizzy is just about to give up when a dark, handsome, virile answer shows up right under her nose. Lizzy may think she and Sarah are going to seduce David—but she underestimates their handsome co-worker, and David turns the tables on them both. But will he be able to tame the untamable Sarah?

Warnings: This title contains graphic language and sex, a m/f/f threesome and mild bdsm elements.

A TWISTED BARD'S TALE
By Selena Kitt

Did you ever wonder what started the feud between the Capulets and the Montagues? Check out this naughty version of Romeo and Juliet - you'll be surprised and delighted by this twisted Bard's tale!

Warning: This title contains graphic language and lesbian sex.

BACK TO THE GARDEN
By Selena Kitt

Discover the deliciously taboo lure of an incestuous siren call with four stories bundled into a wickedly hot anthology that's determined to keep it all in the family!

Warning: This title contains graphic language, sex and mother-son, father-daughter incest.

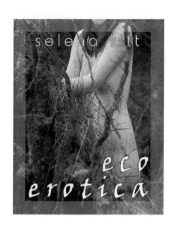

ECOEROTICA
By Selena Kitt

Mother Earth is one hot, sexy Mama, and in this tribute to nature and the environment, Selena Kitt pays homage to her beauty, her grandeur — and her conservation. Who else could tackle topics like global warming, strip mining, animal endangerment and environmental toxicity, all while making it hot, hot, hot?

This anthology includes six sexy and environmentally provocative stories that will rock your world—and arouse and raise more than your environmental awareness. Stories include: The Break, Cry Wolf, Genesis, Law of Conservation, Lightning Doesn't Strike Twice, Paved Paradise,

Warning: This title contains graphic language and sex.

5010822R0

Made in the USA
Lexington, KY
25 March 2010